TOOTHPICK

TOOTHPICK

Kenneth E. Ethridge

Troll Associates

ACKNOWLEDGMENTS

The author would like to express his appreciation and gratitude to fellow writers Michael Barlow and Pat O'Leary for reading and critiquing the manuscript.

A TROLL BOOK, published by Troll Associates, Mahwah, NJ 07430

Published by arrangement with Holiday House, Inc. For information address Holiday House, Inc., 18 East 53rd Street, New York, New York 10022.

First Troll Printing, 1988

Printed in the United States of America.

10 9 8 7 6 5 4 3 2 1

ISBN 0-8167-1316-2

FOR BERNIE, CHRIS, AND ANNA

TOOTHPICK

CHAPTER 1

I can't remember now who came up with the name Tooth-pick for the skinny girl who moved to our town. I mean Toothpick isn't a great name for anyone, but that's how the kids at my school relate to each other. You know—funny names, nicknames, and not-so-funny names.

They call me Needle, short for Needle Legs, although on my school papers you'll see Jamie Almont scrawled at the top. Why Needle? Choosing up sides for volleyball in my first gym class at Glenwood High, a kid shouted, "Hey, you, needle legs! You're on my team." Everybody laughed, and the name wasn't forgotten. At five feet nine, and barely tipping the scales at 130, Mr. T I'm not. It's not that I haven't tried to gain weight, but nothing seems to work.

"Why don't you eat more?" my grandmother asks while piling mashed potatoes on my plate at Sunday dinners. "Your pants look like the American flag flapping around those skinny legs!" A real confidence builder, right?

3

So when I see someone thinner than me, I'm seldom sympathetic. "Boy, is *that* kid skinny!" is what usually goes through my head. I guess you relish the fact that someone is even worse off than you. You know what I mean? Like if a guy with two heads saw somebody else with three, he could feel sort of relieved: "Man, that guy is really weird!"

Harvey Brenhouser, who's my best friend and also quite a wit, could have named Toothpick, but I don't think so.

You can always recognize Harvey. We call him the Pygmy. He's only five feet four, and he wears this dingy air force jacket anywhere and everywhere, all year long. In January or February, when we're freezing our fannies off at the bus stop, that's all he has on besides his street clothes. But even on a stuffy school bus in June, Harvey is still wearing that crumby jacket. I mean the guy is impervious to temperature extremes!

I should point out that Harvey doesn't practice a great deal of personal hygiene. Maybe that provides some sort of insulation from the elements.

Or maybe Rick Lawn gave Toothpick her name. To most of us he's the Beaver. You see, Rick has buck teeth that would make a walrus jealous. When Rick first boarded a Glenwood school bus, somebody said, "Hey, man! Look, it's Bucky Beaver!" A proclamation like that in front of a busload of your classmates can give you a real complex. But that's life at Glenwood High School.

Harvey, Beaver, and I live in the same neighborhood and get picked up at the same bus stop along with a few other kids, so we sort of hang around together. After school we either play cards, Dungeons and Dragons, or war games, or we watch reruns of "The Three Stooges" on the tube. You know, real intellectual stuff.

We usually end up at Harvey's house after the bus ride home. That place seems to be a natural gathering place for lots of creatures. I don't know how many cats the Brenhousers have, but you have to watch your step and where you sit, otherwise you could end up squashing a feline into the sofa or something. That place draws cats like a magnet. They also have a couple of dogs, some fish, and a turtle. But mainly lots of kids.

Harvey is the oldest of about six brothers and sisters. The reason I'm not sure about the number is because the Brenhousers take in foster children. I know the place sounds like a loony bin with all the kids and pets, but everyone seems to feel relaxed and at home. I mean Harvey's mom and dad are really laid back. Nothing seems to phase them.

The first time I visited Harv's, his dad was sprawled on the couch in the living room, jaw hanging open, snoring like crazy. Around him a TV was blaring, the stereo blasted, and some little kids were arguing over how to divvy up a candy bar. I looked sort of shocked, so Harvey explained, "That's my dad. He really knows how to relax." I thought he was in a coma!

But that's the Brenhouser home: very relaxed. You want to stay for dinner? Just set yourself a place and be willing to lend a hand with the dishes. The Brenhousers welcome everyone anytime; they are real homey people.

At my house you practically need an engraved invitation to be allowed in—even if you live there. And Harv, Rick, and I rarely hang around at the Lawns' either. Not that we couldn't—it's just that Harvey's place is a lot more comfortable.

It was during one of those afternoons after school in Harvey's rec room while we were in the middle of our fifth straight game of cutthroat pinochle that the Beaver yawned and announced, "Hey, Jamie, did you see that scrawny-looking chick making googey eyes at you on the bus going home?"

When the three of us are on friendly terms we refer to each other by the names our parents gave us; the nicknames are reserved for a putdown or when we want to be "cool" in front of others.

"You must have been seeing things, Rick," I replied, trying not to appear interested. But the gleam in Beaver's eyes indicated this was more than a joke. Even Harvey perked up.

"Don't tell me Ginger has finally fallen for her secret admirer," Harv said with a knowing smile in my direction.

Harvey and Rick, and not many others, know about my crush on Ginger Gregson. When I was a new transfer student and hopelessly lost on my first day of school, Ginger was the only girl who spoke to me.

"Hi! Are you new here?" she asked with a warm smile. I'll tell you, she knocked my socks off! She was and still is absolutely gorgeous: blond curls, blue eyes, combined with a beautiful personality. But as Harvey said, I was only a secret admirer. Ginger isn't conceited, mind you. She talks to mere mortals like me. But when it comes to purely girl-likes-boy types, she's in the homecoming queen league while I'm an up and coming nerd. So when Rick mentioned a girl being attracted to me, that *was* an unusual occurrence.

"Not Ginger, fool," Rick replied to Harv. "I mean it, Jamie," he continued in earnest, "there was this new girl, a skinny little chick, staring at you like you were Sylvester Stallone or something."

That brought the card game to a halt. The last time a female was attracted to any one of us was last year when Erma Broomgarten fell madly in love with Rick. She thought the Beaver's buck teeth were cute and followed him around everywhere at school.

That might sound only mildly annoying, but Erma weighed about three hundred pounds and wore glasses with lenses about six inches thick. It got so bad, poor Beaver started talking about joining the Foreign Legion or committing suicide. Fortunately, Erma's parents were wealthy and decided she'd benefit from a more exclusive educational experience in the East. They shipped her off to a private school in the fall.

Remembering the Beaver's recent experience with Erma and seeing the sinister smile on his face, I felt uncomfortable.

"She's skinny, huh?" Harvey asked.

"Yeah, like a rake," Beaver continued with relish. "I mean her legs are like this!" He curled his thumb and forefinger into the diameter of a pencil.

"Hey, just your type," Harvey chimed in with a laugh.

"Knock it off, Pygmy," I replied. We rarely refer to Harv by his hated nickname, but he knows how I dislike being reminded of my weight. I have to keep the score even sometimes.

"Come on, man, you know what I mean," Harvey explained. He knew I was getting sore.

"Who wants a little twerp following them around, making googly eyes all the time?" I continued. "That would drive me crazy."

"Hey, I survived my ordeal with Erma," Rick replied. "So now it's your turn."

"Yeah, now you know how Ginger felt the last two years," Harvey said with meaning.

That stopped me cold. I mean I've done some pretty weird things since I've been stuck on Ginger Gregson.

When I was a freshman I sent gobs of anonymous love notes to her and even convinced Harvey to personally deliver one that was over eight pages long. Can you believe it? Over eight pages of mush from some skinny slob she barely knew!

My most dubious achievement, though, was sending a dozen roses to her on her birthday. It was easier to send notes and flowers, since I was too shy to talk to her in person. Whenever she passed me in the hall at school and said something, I would usually respond with infinite maturity: "Uh, yeah. Hi, I mean, ah, what's comin' down, uh . . ." and then, with the gracefulness of a gorilla on crutches, walk into a locker door or trip over a trash can.

You know how it is when you're stuck on someone, but every time they come near you your heart starts pounding, your mouth gets dry, and your face gets hot? I mean I was painfully shy. I'm a quiet person basically, especially around pretty girls; I guess I'm always afraid I'll say something stupid and then look like a klutz.

Once when we were going home on the bus, Ginger sat down next to me. During the twenty-minute ride my palms began sweating, and I started breaking out in hives while I tried to think of something cool to say. By the time we got to our stop I was so uptight I ran all the way home and puked! Man, after that I always made sure I sat next to somebody I felt at ease with.

So when Harvey brought up my affliction with Ginger, and how that made for some awkward moments, he really hit a nerve.

"You guys feel like playing cards anymore?" I asked.

"Nah, my mom's getting on my case because I'm doing so lousy in biology," the Beaver complained. "I guess I'll go home early and look like I'm studying for a while."

"I don't know why you took that class. I told you it was a waste. Swartz is always making you do those retarded reports and then never hands them back. I don't think he even bothers to grade them," Harvey explained with the wisdom of experience.

After a few more caustic remarks about our classes in general, and biology and geometry in particular, we went our separate ways.

When I got home there were assorted pots steaming on the stove, and I could hear my mother scrubbing the bathroom floor. The smell of pot roast, boiled potatoes, and super-strength pine-scented Cleanso Cleaner filled the air.

"Wash your hands downstairs!" was the greeting I heard. "I don't want you tracking through this clean floor!"

My mom has this thing about cleanliness. I think she disinfects the entire house about five times a week. The cleaning isn't so bad, if you don't mind the smell of the great outdoors everywhere. It's the polishing that gets to me. You have to be careful stepping on rugs in the bedrooms. I mean the floors are so slick from about a million coats of wax that a wrong step could dislocate your neck or smash your skull against the wall.

But besides perpetually cleaning, my mother is also a good cook. Pretty soon my dad and I were sitting at the kitchen table while Mom was fixing dinner. He had his nose in the evening paper and was puffing away on his pipe, a habit he acquired in the navy. In between puffs he asked me how the day had gone, which is always kind of weird because he never looks up from his paper while speaking to me.

"How was your day, son?" he'll ask from behind the front page. It's kind of hard to reply to a newspaper headlining the latest leads the police have on a decapitation murder on the other side of the state. I think I could tell him I committed two felonious assaults that afternoon and he'd say, "That's nice. How are you doing in English?"

Still glancing at the business page lying next to his plate, my father mentioned casually, "Met the new neighbors that moved in on Elmhurst today." My dad is a city commissioner or trustee, something like that, but mainly he sells insurance. So he's always friendly when newcomers arrive.

"That's nice, dear," Mom replied, carefully trimming the fat away from a slice of roast.

"Their name's Brooks. Clyde and Thelma. Seem like a nice couple."

"Any children?" my mother asked.

"Only saw one." Dad chanced a quick look in my direction before continuing, "She's skinny as a rail." He's been after me for a long time to put on weight. But his nagging has become more subtle lately. Still, I got the message.

But that wasn't what was bothering me. I was getting the feeling I had heard about this girl before.

"How old is she, Dad?" I ventured.

"About your age, I'd say. You interested?" he said with a sly smile.

I felt my face turning red, and suddenly I didn't feel hungry anymore.

"Thanks for dinner, Mom. I think I'll skip dessert," I muttered, getting up from the table.

"But I made your favorite, devil's food cake!" she exclaimed as I headed down the hall.

"I'm not hungry," I said, closing the bedroom door behind me.

CHAPTER 2

I heard someone say, "Hey, here comes Toothpick," as I got on the bus the next morning. I didn't want to turn around in midstep, so I didn't get a glimpse of her. But while the school bus pulled away, Rick elbowed me in the ribs and whispered hoarsely, "There she is!"

She was skinny, all right. With a white-knuckled hand she gripped a seat back to steady herself before sitting down.

"Well, what do you think?" asked Rick.

I deliberately avoided looking her way and ignored his question. I turned to Harvey and asked him if he had finished our geometry homework.

"What homework?" he asked with a quizzical look.

"Don't be a nerd," I replied in disgust. "We've got homework every night, Harv."

The ride to school was definitely a downer. The February blahs, I guess. Christmas vacation was a distant memory, and all the dirty snow on the ground made Easter seem a

long way off. Summer, ah summer! But that seemed years
away.

First hour's Introduction to Great Literature begins my
day. I don't think there are more than three kids who like
the class. Miss Balkler spends the whole period reading
out loud to us from such thrillers as *Beowulf* and *The Rhyme
of the Ancient Mariner,* written by some old croaker about
nine hundred years ago.

While Old Lady Balkler droned on and on, about half
the class took an early morning nap, while those of us in
the back tried to figure out the geometry assignment due
next hour.

"Can't you worms figure out how to do those easy problems?" Jerome complained. Jerome Humphries, alias the
Hump, lives in our subdivision and rides the same school
bus. The Hump used to hang around with Harv, Rick, and
me, but not anymore. He excels in sports, academic and
romantic pursuits, everything. Meanwhile the runts of the
litter plead hopefully for a little of his wisdom to keep a
passing grade.

"Come on, Hump, just help us with the first set of problems," Skeeter Thomas whined in a whisper.

"All you guys want are the answers," the Hump announced and then laid his head down on the desktop.

I did about half the problems myself; I try to avoid asking
the Hump for help whenever possible. The Beaver's eyes
were shifting from desk to desk. I could tell he was trying
to figure out if Rosie Williams would let him see her paper.
They used to go together in the eighth grade and sometimes

the Beave still cashes in on that.

Mr. Gomez, our second-hour geometry teacher, chewed out Harvey for not having his homework for the third time that week. Harv offered the original excuse that his whole family had stayed up all night praying for his sick aunt in Wichita, but Gomez didn't buy it. After that we got down to the day's allotment of horror-filled problems.

Suddenly the usual doldrums ended when a student entered with a new schedule in hand. I almost went into cardiac arrest! It was Toothpick.

"I'm being switched from Mrs. Hayward's class to yours," she said in a timid voice.

I stared down blankly at the problems we were supposed to be doing. I knew the Beaver and Harvey were giving me wise-guy looks.

"Hey, Needle," a whisper reached me, "looks like your girlfriend's switching into all your classes."

I didn't have to look up to know whose voice it was. The Hump always hits hard in a deadpan voice.

Ever heard the saying "Sticks and stones may break my bones, but words will never hurt me"? My mother used to tell me that gem when I was little and getting teased and picked on all the time. Well, whoever came up with that proverb was either stone deaf or never met any of the kids I go to school with. I could feel my face getting hot, but I just couldn't come up with a cool reply.

Toothpick didn't sit anywhere near me. What a relief! Otherwise I think I would have broken out in hives or worse.

Class continued with me staring at the blank paper on my desk, pretending to be concentrating. When the bell rang I could breathe normally again. I knew she couldn't be in my next class: Boys' Glee Club.

After glee club and gym we ate lunch. Apparently Harvey and Beaver had forgotten about Toothpick joining our math class. They were both arguing about Harvey's great-grandfather, Erwin von Brenhouser. Harvey claims his ancestor was a World War I flying ace and shot down as many planes as the famous Red Baron. I guess it's possible; he's got some pictures and medals, and some fancy papers written in German. But Beaver claims it's just a figment of Harv's overactive imagination.

"I'm telling you, my grandmother can read German, and she'll tell ya he was really her father when she sees us over Easter!" Harvey argued, his mouth full of one of the cafeteria's recyclable hot dogs. We think someday the Surgeon General will put warnings on the food served in school lunches.

"Yeah, Harv. You told us that last year, and she never showed up," Rick replied.

As I sat down to my three ice-cream sandwiches and an order of tator tots—I firmly believe in a balanced diet—Beaver casually offered, "Aren't you going to look for Janice?"

"What?"

"Janice Brooks—Toothpick," he explained with a smile.

"Boy, you must really like her to have already asked for her name," I replied, trying to turn the tables on him.

"Huh-uh, Jamie Boy, she's got the hots for you, not me.

I just asked Sally Heinz in the office who the new girl was,"
Beaver continued, staring at me with this retarded grin on
his face.

What was I suppose to say? Gee, thanks a lot, Rick. Now
that I know her name I can ask her out.

I just gave him the most putrid look I could manage and
started eating my lunch. But the day's events made the
cafeteria's delicacies more tasteless than usual.

Toothpick showed up in only one more of my classes:
Art and Music Appreciation, the last class of the day. Fortunately, Harv, Rick, and the Hump don't appreciate art
or music and aren't in that class, so I knew I wouldn't get
razzed.

Once during class, when I glanced in her direction, I
wondered just who was this creature who supposedly found
me so irresistible. She looked at me at the same time and
our eyes met. She smiled in an odd sort of way, like she
was unsure of herself. I quickly looked above her head at
the wall clock and then glanced at my wrist, pretending I
was checking my watch. The trouble was, I don't wear a
watch. Melanie Evans, who was watching my bizarre be-
havior, asked, "What time is it? Half past a freckle, Eastern
Elbow Time?"

Melanie uses humor that was considered cool during
caveman times, so I just ignored the remark, but began
feeling badly about not having smiled back at Toothpick. I
mean, I could remember two years ago when I first transferred here. It's tough getting used to a new school. "I
could have smiled back," I half said to myself.

I didn't look her way again. Before long the bell rang,

and everybody was making their way to their lockers and then to the mud-splattered yellow buses lined up in the parking lot.

I got on good old number 24 and sat down next to Skeeter Thomas.

"Hey, Skeeter, you understand that geometry stuff we're working on?" I asked.

"Are you kiddin', man? I'm flunkin' that class for sure this marking period. My old man will croak unless I get a decent grade. And if I don't, I can forget about baseball."

Skeeter's a little guy, but he's the best second-baseman at Glenwood and could win his varsity letter this year if it wasn't for our stupid math class.

"Hey, Hump!" he shouted, bounding over my legs. "No basketball practice tonight?"

"It got canceled."

As the Hump took his seat, Skeeter began pleading for some help in geometry. I knew Jerome would come through; he's the team's first-baseman and wants Skeeter playing baseball this spring, too.

Meanwhile I sat alone. Harv and Beaver were in one of the back seats yakking about who was going to win in a new game Harvey got in the mail. Then I noticed Toothpick outside, wandering from bus to bus, looking for the right number. I felt sorry for her. You could tell she wasn't sure which one was ours.

Finally she got on board and looked relieved at the sight of some vaguely familiar faces. I forgot there weren't many empty seats handy, and when the bus started creaking and rolling away, she sort of plopped down next to me. I mean,

I don't think she was looking for me to sit next to.

"Hello," she said cheerfully, but all out of breath. "I didn't think I would find the bus in time," she explained in earnest; you could tell she'd been afraid of being left behind.

The way she said it, so matter-of-factly, made me relax a little. She wasn't trying to be cool like the rest of us pretend to do all the time, you know, when we look stupid or scared.

"My name's Janice—Janice Brooks," she said, this time a little timidly.

I almost blurted out, "Yeah, I know!" I'm not much when it comes to social graces. I just sat there, kicking at a glob of petrified bubble gum on the floor. Finally, I managed to introduce myself, and pretty soon we were talking about the complicated business of moving into a new house and getting used to a new school.

I told her about my second day of school when we first moved in; I got the bus numbers confused and got on number 42 instead of 24. Forty-two took me to the wrong part of town, and I had to walk in the rain to a phone booth and call my mom. She sent a taxi that finally brought me home. Janice laughed hard—but not at me. She told how today in the lunch line she hit the straw dispenser too hard and about forty-seven straws rolled into her bowl of chili. That really cracked me up. We laughed so loud a couple of times, I noticed Hump and Skeeter turn around and give us funny looks.

She was easy to talk to. She told me she felt like a klutz most of the time, too.

"You should see my father," she explained. "He's always

bumping his head or knees on something. But whenever he does anything clumsy, he just laughs it off. He always tells me, 'Never forget to laugh at yourself!' So that's what I try to do."

I remember thinking how strange that seemed—laughing at yourself. It seemed like Harv, Beaver, and I were always thinking of things to put down or poke fun at about each other—never about ourselves.

When we got off the bus I felt a little awkward. We stood there just a moment before she said, "It sure was nice meeting you, Jamie. I'll see you later." She had a real warm smile. Then she walked toward her street, and I debated whether I should try to catch up with Harv and Rick, who were already heading for Harvey's place.

I quickened my pace and was soon walking beside them. When Beaver saw me he gave a broad, bucktoothed smile. "Ah! So I see you're wasting no time making your move, Jamie."

When I sort of hung my head down with a sullen look, Harvey put his hand on my shoulder and said with mock sympathy, "Aw-w-w, man, don't be ashamed. But you gotta remember, Ginger's gonna be brokenhearted now that you've found someone else."

I brushed his hand off and said, "You guys are really screwy. Just because the girl happens to sit next to me and we have a little conversation, you make it out to be a big deal."

"Come on, Jamie. We're your friends. We understand. Everybody needs somebody," Harv replied with a stupid grin on his face.

"Yeah, Jamie," Beaver continued, "we'll keep your romance a secret. Won't we, Harv?"

"You know, Bucky Beaver," I said slowly, "sometimes you take things a little too far. I don't care for that skinny little twerp, and I'm not madly in love with anybody."

Like I said before, we save the nicknames for a putdown. Rick turned red when I said "Bucky Beaver," and the sly smile disappeared from his face. He could see I was getting ticked off.

"Come on, you guys." Harv tried to smooth things over. "She's just a skinny little twerp like Jamie said. There ain't no use gettin' bent out of shape over it."

"That's right. I don't care about your love life, Needle," the Beaver had to say—getting even.

"Well, if I hustle a little, I'll make it home in time to watch the Stooges," I announced, beginning to cut across a vacant lot that's a shortcut to my house.

"Hey, man, what're you so sore about? What about the game?" Harv cried after me.

"You got Beaver to play it with!" I shouted over my shoulder.

"Yeah, but it's better with three guys!" Harvey continued.

I guess I was in no mood to play a new war game or another version of Dungeons and Dragons. I just walked home.

"I thought you were going to Harvey's house," my mother greeted me as I came in the door—disappointed at seeing me home so early.

"I didn't feel like it."

"What's wrong with you three now?" she asked.

"Nothing, Ma. Can I have a piece of that cake we had last night?"

"You can have some cookies," she replied.

Equipped with a glass of milk and a handful of Double Fudge Delights, I parked in front of the TV and flicked on the familiar strains of "Three Blind Mice." Good old Larry, Moe, and Curly would help take my mind off the day.

"Don't get crumbs on anything, I just vacuumed!"

"OK, Ma."

CHAPTER 3

I took Benny for a walk after we ate supper. Benny's our arthritic basset hound who's about twelve years old. I figured out what that was in human years once. You know, each dog year is worth so many human years. Anyway, the way I figured it, Benny should be in a wheelchair or an old folks' home for dogs by now. But he's like part of the family, and none of us can stand the thought of getting rid of him. I know one day he'll head for that big dog kennel in the sky, but meanwhile I still need him around.

Those walks down the road at night with Benny always give me time to think. When I look in the windows of different houses and see the silver glare from TV sets, I get the feeling I'm totally removed from the world and all its hassles.

This thing about Toothpick was getting me down. I mean, who should care who I talk to or who talks to me? Sometimes going to Glenwood High feels like living in a goldfish bowl; everybody watches everyone else and keeps close tabs on your personal affairs. Maybe I should say your fears, phobias, or handicaps—whatever you want to call them— are closely examined by everyone.

Harvey called me after I got back from walking my dog.

"Hey, that game is no fun without a third guy playing," he complained.

I knew what he was really trying to say: "Gee, I hope there's no hard feelings." Only he wouldn't come right out and say *that*. He just droned on and on about how this new game worked and how much I would really like it.

I started doodling on the note pad hanging near the phone and occasionally mumbled, "Yeah, Harv, uh-huh."

"You wanna come over or somethin'?" he finally asked.

"Not tonight, Harv. I'm not in the mood for fighting with tanks or dragons."

"There's a new movie on cable TV," he tried to tempt me. "It's called *Thoran the Terrible*. I bet I can talk my mom into letting us watch it." I knew then that Harvey really wanted to make amends. His parents are kind of religious, see, so it's a really big deal if Harv can talk them into letting him and a friend watch an R-rated movie.

"Thanks anyway, Harv. But I don't think so tonight."

"Whatsa matter? You still sore at me and Beaver?"

"No, no. I just don't feel like seein' anybody, that's all. I'm not sore at anybody. Listen," I went on, "we'll get together tomorrow night for a game. OK?"

"Anything you say," Harv replied unenthusiastically. "I'll see ya tomorrow, huh?"

"OK, Harv."

But I *was* sore at somebody. I just couldn't figure out who or why. Maybe I was mad at myself for what I had said about Toothpick. I guess I didn't want to get caught up in some kind of mess where it looked like I was defending this skinny little girl. Maybe that sounds cruel, but I believe in the survival of the fittest. I'm not a tough guy, and I couldn't see putting myself between Toothpick and people like the Beaver or Hump or anybody else who really decided to razz her.

Still, the whole thing bothered me. Even though my dad always says, "It's a dog-eat-dog world, son; you gotta get used to it," I wondered how I should act, or what I would say the next time some wise guy said something to her or me.

I remembered an incident last year that involved Arnold Sherwinberger. I'm serious—that's really the guy's name. But everybody at school calls him Cheeseburger. It would have been bad enough living with a name like that, but Arnold also carries a lunch box and thermos with him every day, and his wardrobe is strictly Salvation Army specials.

Cheeseburger is the target of a lot of guys. They not only call him names, they really do some rotten things. One day I was on the second floor near the boys' john when four of our more illustrious tough guys were carrying Arnold inside, intending to give him a "swirly"—you know, dunk his head in and flush. I thought maybe I could run for a teacher—I didn't want to end up in a wheelchair or something trying to stop it myself. But before I could move, I was practically trampled by Glenwood's answer to the Incredible Hulk: Norris Pendowski.

Norris plays center on the football team and works a jackhammer for his dad's construction company in the summer, so without any trouble he got one guy by the collar and a shorter one by the hair and slammed them both into the lockers.

"Whatsa matter with youse guys?" he roared. "Enough's enough! Leave the guy alone!"

After the cool dudes explained they were just "kiddin' around" and took off, I tried to thank Norris for stopping it.

"It ain't right," he scowled and then walked away.

And that's how I felt about Toothpick: "It ain't right."

When I was walking down the street the next morning, a car horn blared, and in the old clunker he and his dad had been working on, Hump tore down the pavement, stinking up the environment with clouds of exhaust fumes. The Hump on wheels—what's the world coming to? I could see him laugh after I leaped out of the way. Such a warmhearted person, I said to myself. I knew none of us who lived near him could expect a ride to school; that honor would be reserved for varsity club members only. But as I trudged down the street I consoled myself with the thought that whenever Jerome drove his car he wouldn't be riding the bus, so some of us would endure fewer put-downs on the ride to school.

"Did you see the Hump in that crazy car?" Beaver asked as I got to the bus stop. He was all smiles, apparently forgiving our heated exchange from the day before.

"I'm surprised the thing even runs," I said.

"Don't worry," Harv put in, "if the car breaks down, Hump'll make the Amazon get out and push." A few others standing around us laughed at Harvey's remark as the bus pulled up. "The Amazon" is Harvey's nickname for Patricia Humphries, Jerome's younger sister. Although she's only a freshman, she's already about as tall as her big brother. Next to Harv, she really *does* look like an Amazon.

The bus pulled away, and I didn't notice Toothpick anywhere. The ride to school was almost pleasant: the sun was shining, Hump wasn't around with his usual sarcastic remarks, and Rick and Harvey seemed to have forgotten about Toothpick.

CHAPTER 4

As it turned out, Toothpick missed a lot of school; she was absent at least once or twice a week. Still, she always had her homework up to date, even in math, where Mr. Gomez piles it on.

"I wish my mom and dad would let me take so many days off," Harv complained one day in a whisper, his head cradled lazily in his arms on top of the desk. We were staring out the window during sociology, trying to keep awake during a filmstrip. It was a real thriller: *Social Interaction among Pygmies*.

"Are you kiddin', Harv? If you missed that many days you'd never finish high school!" Beaver pointed out. "Do you ever see the papers she gets back?" he continued. "All A's."

"Yeah," Harvey muttered, "I bet her old man does it for her."

But Toothpick's father didn't do her homework; she had

a skinny bod but a king-sized brain. I found that out a short time after we met.

For a while I didn't have a whole lot to say to Toothpick. Don't get the wrong idea. I wasn't unfriendly; I was just sort of . . . you know, careful. It seemed like half the time she was gone anyway, and when I did see her, I'd smile and say, "Hi."

Janice was always friendly, though. She not only said hello, she'd always ask, "How are you?" and when she said it you could tell she really wanted to know. That bothered me at first. You know how some people ask you how you're doing, but they could care less? My aunt Harriet's like that; she'll say, "Oh, how are you, Jamie?" and before I can answer she's onto the next question. Just once I'd like to answer, "I've got an advanced case of galloping athlete's foot, Aunt Harriet," but I doubt if she'd even notice.

But when Janice asked how I was, she really meant it. That's how I found out she was so good in math.

One day while we were boarding the bus to go home, I noticed Janice sitting by herself in one of the front seats. We had sat together a couple of times already, but it was always Janice who joined me. To be honest, I was still afraid of being razzed by someone. Rick and Harvey hadn't said much about "you and Toothpick" lately, except an occasional wink or a sly grin when she passed us in the hall, but I was still careful. Seeing Janice sitting alone and giving me her usual warm smile, I just couldn't walk by.

As I flopped down in the seat next to her, I asked, "How's it goin'?"

"I'm doing fine. How about you?" She never failed to

give me that sincere look.

"I guess I'm no good in math," I blurted out, speaking what was really on my mind instead of the usual "Oh, not bad." I had gotten a five-week progress report from Mr. Gomez that morning. Along with seven others, I was informed that I was failing geometry and had five more weeks, until the marking period ended, to clean up my act.

With some teachers you can throw the reports away; they either forget to ask for them back or, I suppose, could care less. But with Gomez you have to return them with your parents' signature.

For Harvey, who got progress reports the first two marking periods, it was no problem—he's an expert at forging his dad's signature. He even adds little comments like "I'm grounding Harvey for a week so he will shape up this time."

But I can't do that. I guess I'm not afraid of getting caught as much as having to explain to my folks why I'm failing and why I hadn't told them before.

When I mentioned the problem to Janice, she was really sympathetic.

"Couldn't your mom or dad help you out?" she asked as the bus lurched out of the parking lot.

"Nah. They're not up on the latest math. Anyway, I got a C and a D the first two marking periods, so I don't think Gomez will flunk me for the year."

"Would you like someone to help you out?" she asked.

I knew what was coming next. I hesitated and said, "Yeah . . . I guess so."

"Well, how about coming over to my house after supper tonight? My dad is great in math, and he helps me if I get stuck. He's an engineer and can explain things really well. I was never any good in math until he started helping me."

So there I was. I could feel my face starting to get hot, wondering what to say.

"Well . . . yeah, I guess so."

"Good!" She smiled back. "What time should I expect you?"

"Ah . . ." I was sort of paralyzed by this time, and I wondered if anyone nearby had heard her invitation. But with the usual shouting and laughing, and with Wilma, our bus driver, grinding through the gears, there wasn't much chance.

"Listen, you can just call me after supper and let me know when's a good time. OK?"

I couldn't make much conversation the rest of the way home, even though Janice had a few things to say.

"This is my number," she said quietly and shoved a tiny folded piece of paper into my hand as we came to our stop. I quickly stuffed it in my pocket. Good grief! I thought, what if she had waited until we were all standing up, waiting to get off, and everybody had heard her?

"I'll see you later, Jamie," she said cheerfully as we started down different streets to our homes.

Beaver looked back at her and then flashed his buck teeth in a nasty grin. But after I gave him a dirty look, he wiped the smile off his face.

"Hey, Harvey, when's your old lady gonna' give in and let us watch *Thoran?*" Rick asked.

"I told ya before, if my folks go to that prayer meeting tonight we can see it then."

"But you said it starts at eight-thirty. When do your folks get back?"

"Sometimes as late as ten."

"But the movie's two hours long, Harv," the Beaver complained. "What are we gonna do, watch half of a movie?"

"Hey, man, that's the best I can do!"

"Well, do we go?" Beave asked, looking my way.

"I don't know if I can make it," I said.

"What? You don't wanna see *Thoran?*" Harvey cried. Rick stared at me too, a funny look on his face.

"It's not that I don't wanna see it. It's just—" I kept trying to think of a good excuse. "Well, what do you think my mom and dad are gonna say when I show them my five-week report in math?"

"Same as always, Jamie," Rick replied. "'You just do your best, son, that's all we ask.'" Rick does a pretty good imitation of my father's voice. Rick and Harvey both know my parents don't throw a spasm when I get a rotten grade in a tough subject.

"I don't know about that," I continued. "First a C, then a D, and now I'm flunkin' the class."

We trudged along in silence before Harvey reasoned, "Maybe if you don't come over now, they'll let you come tonight."

"Yeah, I think you're right," I said. "Listen, I'll call you after supper and let you know what the deal is."

My folks don't freak out when I give them bad news about my scholastic ability, or lack of it. Dad will usually look at me quietly, puffing away on his pipe. And Mom folds her hands and looks like she's quietly counting to ten—the way she did the time I dropped her favorite flower vase on the kitchen floor, smashing it into a million pieces. Although *that* time her eyes sort of went back in her head, and she got real pale, like she was going to faint!

After supper, my parents usually sit at the kitchen table drinking coffee and reading the evening paper. So around seven I dialed Harvey's number and quickly thought of how to turn down his invitation. With our phone in the kitchen, my plan worked easily.

When one of the little kids at the Brenhouser home finally found Harvey, I explained the situation.

"Harv," I said quietly, trying to sound really down. "I can't make it tonight."

"Whatsa matter? They really lay into you about it?"

"Yeah," I replied. I felt a little uncomfortable with my dad peering at me over the editorial page.

"They in the room now?" Harvey asked; he was aware of my parents' habits and the location of our phone.

"Yeah, I better tell you about it later." My father's eyes widened a bit. "I'll see ya."

"OK, Jamie."

I wasn't about to call Janice with my parents sitting there, so I went into my room for a while. I flopped down on the bed and stared at the ceiling, listening to the air pump bubbling in my aquarium.

After their coffee, my parents go into the living room for a couple of hours of TV. When they did, I sneaked back into the kitchen and stared at the telephone.

"Oh! You scared me," my mother cried bumping into me after she entered the darkened kitchen.

"Sorry, Ma."

"What are you doing? I thought you were in your bedroom." She always likes to ask two- or three-part questions.

"I gotta make a phone call."

"Well, go ahead," she replied, giving me a suspicious look.

After I dialed, the phone didn't even finish ringing once before Janice answered.

"Hello?"

"Hi, Janice. It's me—I mean it's Jamie."

She chuckled at my awkwardness, but I didn't feel insulted. We talked for a couple of minutes, and I agreed to come over.

"I'm goin' out," I announced to my parents, who were still sitting in the living room.

"Where to?" my dad asked, lowering his newspaper. He'd finally worked his way to the sports page.

"Just over to a friend's to do some homework."

"Can you tell us who, son?" he had to ask. My mother was also staring at me now. The only sound in the room was coming from the grandfather clock.

"Janice Brooks's," I said reluctantly.

"Oh! Well, have a good time." They looked at each other, then back at me with goofy smiles on their faces. I knew they meant well, but I felt weird. You know, "Well, he's finally got a girlfriend," or something really strange was probably going through their heads.

I trotted over to Janice's house as fast as I could because I was afraid I might run into the Hump or maybe Rick coming back from Harvey's. It probably sounds like I was really embarrassed about being seen at her house. Well, to tell the truth, I was!

I knocked on the door, wondering what to expect. I stood there hoping Janice would be the one who answered the door.

She did, and she was all smiles when I walked in.

Her mom and dad were pretty nice. They were friendly but didn't force you into conversation or look as if they wished you'd dry up and blow away like some parents do.

We started working on our math homework at the kitchen table while her parents disappeared into another room. After a while I started to relax. Janice was more than just pleasant. It seemed like she was happy or excited about everything: school, the pukey weather; she even liked our teachers—that really freaked me out.

"I love Mr. Pitts's class, don't you?"

"It's OK, I guess," was my reply.

"Don't you like classical music?"

"Some of it's all right. I mean I liked that thing he played yesterday."

"Oh, you mean the piano concerto?"

Piano concerto! Can you believe it? I don't even know what one is. But that was Janice; she liked *everything*.

But she did help me with my math problems; in about thirty minutes we were finished. After that she asked me if I wanted to listen to some music. What could I say?

They must have had over two hundred albums in their living room.

"Are these all yours?"

"Oh no. A lot of them are my cousin's—he gave them

to me. And some are my mom and dad's."

She had a little bit of everything. Classical, jazz, country, but mainly good old rock and roll.

"The Beatles!" I exclaimed. "I've never seen all their albums together before."

"My cousin's," Janice explained.

I picked out something a little less ancient, and she put it on the turntable.

We sat there for over an hour, just talking and listening to a few albums. Like I said before, she was really easy to talk to.

"Did you get used to Glenwood very quickly?"

"Well...no!" I answered honestly.

"What happened?" she asked, with that concerned look in her eyes.

"I don't think I talked to anybody for a couple of weeks. I was kinda lonely. I mean, I'm sorta shy, and that didn't help either."

"Who finally broke the ice?"

"Believe it or not, Ginger Gregson was the first person to really talk to me."

"Ginger?" Janice replied. "She *is* nice."

"Yeah. I guess she felt sorry for me. But my first good friend at school was Harvey."

"That short guy you sit with on the bus?"

"Yeah. It's funny; Harvey practically forced himself on me."

"Tell me," she said with a smile.

I laughed, thinking back to that time. "Well, Harv *is* kinda different. He tried to start conversations with me at the bus stop, but I kinda shyed away. You know—who's this weird little guy?"

Janice laughed.

"Anyway, one day I was walking my dog, Benny, out in some woods away from our house when I heard this voice: 'Hey! Hey, wait up!' It was Harv."

"He followed you out to the woods?" Janice asked in amazement.

"Yeah. I remember he was wearing that crazy jacket he always wears. He came running up to me and said, 'Hey, I just wanna be your friend, man.' And we've been friends since then."

"That's sweet." She smiled, then began to cough. She had been coughing every now and then, and I figured she had a cold or sore throat; but then she started coughing so hard she had to excuse herself from the room. While Janice was getting cough medicine or something, her mother came in and offered me a Coke.

I was enjoying a glass of pimple pusher when Janice returned and made herself a cup of tea with milk. Doesn't that make you want to gag? Anyway, she said that's how the British take their tea.

"It sounds awful, doesn't it?" she asked as I stared at her concoction.

"Well . . . yeah!" I admitted, and then we both started laughing.

"It's all right. I use to think it was pretty bad, too." She was so honest and cheerful at the same time.

"Are you making many friends?" I asked. It seemed like most of the time we talked about me or my problems, so

I was trying to be polite.

"In some of my classes," she said softly.

"Maybe it's hard to, I mean, you being absent a lot." After I said that Janice got this sad look on her face. Thatta boy, Almont, I thought; open mouth and insert foot.

"I—I didn't mean anything," I stammered.

"That's OK, Jamie," she told me. "I do get sick a lot."

She sat there silently staring into her teacup. I must have hit a nerve or something. I mean Janice was always so cheerful, and suddenly it was gloom city.

"A person can't help if they're sick," I offered. "My aunt Dorothy had to move to Arizona because of her asthma," I continued. "She had a tough time every winter until she moved."

"Asthma's a respiratory disease. Like I have." Janice said.

"You've got asthma?" I asked.

"No. It's called cystic fibrosis. I was born with it," she explained, still staring at her tea.

"Citric . . . what?"

Janice smiled a little. "I know it's hard to pronounce." She looked up at my puzzled expression. "It's a respiratory disease. My lungs get clogged with a lot of gunk—that's why I cough so much. And I have to take vitamins and special enzymes to keep things working right." She spoke so softly I knew it had to be serious, even if I didn't know what it was.

"Doesn't sound like fun."

"It's not. That's why I miss so many days of school. I get sick a lot, and then I have to take tons of antibiotics and wait till I'm better."

I didn't stay much longer after that. I guess I didn't know what else to say. Mr. and Mrs. Brooks said good-bye and told me to come again.

They seemed as nice as Harvey's parents; not as laid back, maybe, but just as kind.

When I got ready to leave, Janice told me to let her know whenever I needed help in math.

As I walked home, I thought about Janice and that strange-sounding illness. It must be tough, I thought. Yet she always seemed so cheerful and positive. When I walked up our driveway, a thought entered my mind and stayed with me: Janice must be really brave.

"Get all your homework done?" my father asked when I came in.

"Yeah."

I knew he wanted to ask me about Toothpick, but I just walked to my room and closed the door. No sense in trying to explain. If I said we were only friends, he'd just grin and say, "Well, you always start out as friends."

Let them figure it out, I thought.

CHAPTER 5

The next morning I wondered if Toothpick would mention my visit to anyone at school. I didn't have to worry, though; she was absent again. And for the first time, her being gone bothered me.

When I was sitting with Harvey and Rick during lunch, I noticed how negative they were about everything.

"Hey, Harvey, did you see that new kid in gym?" Beaver asked, a wicked grin on his face.

"You mean the one with all the zits?" Harv asked.

"Yeah! Jamie, you should see this guy. I mean he's got pimples on his arms, his back, his—"

"Lay off it, Rick," I interrupted. "The guy's got a problem. So don't make fun."

"Who's makin' fun?" the Beaver cried. "I'm just tellin' you about this weird dude!"

"I don't wanna hear it, man!"

"OK, OK. Jeez, what's the matter with you?" he continued.

"Your parents still sore?" Harvey asked.

"Nah. Forget it." But it was hard listening and not knowing what to say.

When Harvey bragged about suckering in Mr. Gomez with his third forged progress report, I just stared at someone's half-eaten chili dog. A fly hovered nearby, probably trying to figure out if it was edible or a close relative of Agent Orange. But when Rick said I had a substitute teacher in Art and Music Appreciation, I had to ask, "Who's the sub?"

"Star Wars!" he said with a laugh and flash of buck teeth. "Don'tcha remember?" he continued. "She subbed for Gomez about a month ago."

"Yeah, I remember." While Rick and Harvey roared, I recalled the rotten way our math class treated the substitute teacher Hump had named Star Wars. You know, spaced out, not all there. I guess the name was appropriate. I mean, we've had some strange subs before, but this lady was a basket case.

When she came into our math class second hour, she was carrying a mug of coffee, and her glasses kept sliding down her nose. She tried to take attendance using the roster from another class.

While she kept calling out the wrong names, Hump said loud enough for everyone to hear, "Man, is this chick weird or what?"

With everyone giggling and making faces at her, she went

to the room phone and called the office. "The students are not answering me while I take roll!" she told one of the secretaries in a high-pitched voice.

Everyone cracked up at that point. I mean it really *was* funny. Finally, Mrs. Meisner, one of the secretaries, came to the room and straightened her out.

When she finally got the right class list, everyone answered her in a high-pitched voice, trying to mimic hers. We must've driven her nuts, because when Gomez got back he read us the riot act.

She didn't do much better that day in Art and Music Appreciation. I guess a screwy sub can bring out the worst in your personality. Even a guy like Leonard Pitkin, who's so well behaved that Hump calls him Dudley Do-Good, loses control.

While she was writing some things on the board, Leonard and Sally Heinz gave the signal for everyone to drop their books on the floor. The music room has a really high ceiling, so throwing something heavy on the floor echoes loudly, and about forty books at once sound like a major earthquake.

Through it all, I kept thinking of Toothpick. You know, how she would react to the situation. I couldn't help thinking that she'd be turned off by what was happening. I was confused. Normally I didn't care, but she liked this class, the way she seemed to like everything, and I thought she'd be really bummed out by what was going on.

When we went home, the kids on the bus who were in that class talked about it with everyone. I thought about

Arnold, the Cheeseburger, and the way Norris Pendowski had stopped those guys from giving him a swirly. Norris had said it wasn't right, and I guess we hadn't done right with Star Wars. I mean, she got paid for it and everything, but somehow it didn't seem fair, driving somebody crazier than they already were.

Beave, Harvey, and I spent the afternoon in Harvey's rec room playing Galactic Invaders on the video game the Brenhousers have. We really got into it, and I forgot about everything for a while. We actually played through the Stooges, which doesn't happen very often.

It had been a while since I'd horsed around with those guys; even the Hump came by after practice, and we played two on two. Things were going great. But just when we were getting ready to walk out the door, Mrs. Brenhouser made a casual remark that sort of changed things from then on.

"Jamie, I was grocery shopping today, and Thelma Brooks said you were getting some help in math from her daughter, Janice. I wish I could talk Harvey into getting some help in geometry."

It was an offhand remark, that's all, but you can imagine the way the guys looked at me.

"Uh-oh. Sounds like Jamie's been spendin' time with his chicky-poo," the Beaver announced.

"Well, James, seems like you've been holdin' out on us," said the Hump—always trying to sound like an adult when he's around our parents. I knew he'd have more to say later.

Mrs. Brenhouser saw me turn red, and I knew she regretted having said anything.

"I'm sorry, Jamie," she began, "I didn't know..."

"Forget it, Mrs. Brenhouser." I ducked out the door in a hurry.

"What do you see in that skinny little chick?" Beaver asked as he and Harv followed me down the driveway.

"She asked me if I wanted help in math, stupid. I went over to her house, and she helped. She's good in math. That's all there is to it."

"You sure?" Beaver asked with just a slight smile. He likes to pretend he's being serious or helpful sometimes, when all he's trying to do is set you up for a putdown.

"I like her as much as you liked Erma," I replied.

The only thing preventing me from slugging him, or using some choice words which would have made him slug me, was Harvey.

"I'm tired of hearin' about it, Rick," Harvey put in as we reached the street. "Let's just leave it alone, huh?" I walked the rest of the way home by myself.

Harvey isn't the most sensitive person in the world, yet deep down he's a decent sort of guy. A little weird, maybe, though decent. That night he called me and said, "Hey, don't get me wrong, Jamie, but what is it between you and Toothpick?"

"We're friends, Harv. Is that OK with you or what?" I asked sarcastically.

"Hey, *I'm* your friend, too, OK? I'm not layin' into ya like the Beaver."

It was true, he wasn't. The problem, I guess, was that

I still felt uncomfortable with the whole idea of being friends with Janice. That sounds cruel, doesn't it? But all I wanted to do was get along in the world.

A few weeks or so after I had first gone over to Janice's house, she called me on the phone.

"Jamie, it's for you!" my dad hollered from the kitchen.

We had eaten supper earlier, but my parents were still at the kitchen table with their coffee and newspapers.

"Hello," I mumbled in response to Janice's cheery greeting. I kept my back to my folks. I knew they'd hear every word, but I just didn't feel like watching them listen.

"Jamie, I'd like to talk to you about something." She just left it at that and didn't say anything else.

"What, Janice?"

"Do you think you could come over?"

"Ah . . . OK. I'll be there in a few minutes."

I didn't give my parents any song and dance, I just said, "I'm going over to Janice's for a while."

I wondered what was on her mind as I trudged over to her house. I kept thinking she might say she was madly in love with me or something like that, and then I'd probably croak on the spot. I just couldn't figure how all this got started.

When I got there, she asked me to come into the living room, and we sat down together on a couch. I was a little nervous. You know, like what if her parents were listening to every word? But Janice did most of the talking.

"I'm sorry about what's happened," she began.

"What do you mean?"

"I'm afraid it looks like people have been saying that we're . . . you know, attached to each other." She didn't say "going together," I thought with relief. "And I know you don't feel that way," she continued in a real soft voice, still sort of smiling.

"Yeah, I guess so," I said.

"I really respect you a lot," she said, "and I want us to stay friends. But I don't want to embarrass you in any way." She understood, I thought.

"I think we can still be friends, Janice," I said.

After that we talked, and talked, and talked some more. I told her how Harvey, Rick, and I all hung around together. After a while I explained the nicknames to her. She laughed when I told her how Beaver got his nickname and his trials with Erma last year.

Then I told her my nickname was Needle and how the Hump had come up with that name to describe my "needle legs."

"But you aren't skinny, Jamie," she said seriously.

"Are you kiddin'? Maybe not to you, but I am to everybody else."

"Does it really matter what other people say or think about you?" she asked.

"Well . . . yeah," I said honestly.

"Jamie, the thinnest person in the whole school is me. But I can't let that get me down." She kept getting to me with that warm smile.

I thought how brave she was to admit her handicaps or weaknesses, whatever you want to call them, so openly.

"You know, Janice, you're pretty tough for a skinny kid.

You know what I mean?"

"I know what you mean," she replied with a smile. "You're a pretty strong person, too, even if you don't realize it."

And that's how we always talked. Like I was someone special. It almost sounds like she was trying to psych me out or something, but she wasn't really.

When I left her house that night, I had a different feeling about her. I really did begin to look at her as a friend. And I felt something else that I had never felt before, except with my parents and maybe Harvey: I felt like I could trust Janice. Does that make sense? I don't know how many people you *really* trust with your feelings or whatever's on your mind, but for me it hasn't been many. With Janice, I realized I could tell her my deepest thoughts.

CHAPTER 6

We didn't see each other every day. Like I said before, Janice was sick a lot. But usually we got together once or twice a week in her kitchen to do math.

Harvey and Rick didn't care for my new pal. Harvey wasn't bothered too much; it was the Beaver who gave me the most hassle. Finally, I told them both never to mention Toothpick around me again. Harvey said OK, and I got Beaver in line when I threatened to write a letter to good old Erma, telling her that Rick was madly in love and couldn't live another day without her. We all knew that Erma, all three hundred pounds of her, would have hopped on the next flight and probably parachuted into the Beaver's front yard.

Hump razzed me occasionally, but with spring approaching, his car seemed to run almost every day, so he wasn't on the bus very often to pass on those cherished words of wisdom.

Meanwhile, my grades in math began to go up, and by the time the third marking period ended I got a B minus in geometry. I know that doesn't sound too awesome, but for *me* it was nothing short of a miracle.

The reason why my grades went up, of course, was Janice's doing. We didn't just do math when we got together, though; we also talked a lot and listened to music.

Remembering back, it seems like most of the time we talked about me. Janice didn't seem to mind, and she had such a positive way of looking at life, in spite of her illness, that it made me want to talk about anything and everything.

Like my crush on Ginger Gregson. I was able to tell her all about that, and she didn't crack up like Harv and Rick had. In fact, she seemed to understand and make some things clear to me that I didn't realize before.

"You were trying too hard, that's all," she explained.

"Say what?" I replied.

"Jamie, you liked her so much and wanted so badly to say the right thing that you ended up getting real uptight and saying the wrong things. You just weren't yourself. With me you're talkative, funny, and the thing I like most about you: you're sincere."

"Sincere, huh?" I answered, but I guess I didn't really understand what she meant.

"You'd be surprised," she went on. "Ginger thinks the guy she's dating now is a big flake."

"Are you kiddin' me?" I cried.

"Not at all."

"Ginger told you that Joe Pentatella is a flake?" I asked in amazement. I remember Harvey saying not long ago that

Ginger went with Pentatella because he was the only guy with the nerve to ask her out. But Joe and Ginger seemed to be the perfect match to everybody: in looks, personality, and all the other good stuff that makes you one of the "in" crowd.

"We're lab partners in chemistry. She tells me lots of things," Janice explained.

"I bet you'd be surprised how people would act toward you if you didn't worry so much about what they might think," she said gently.

And Janice was right. One day as Harvey, Rick, and I were going through the lunch line, the Beaver tried to make me look like a fool while Ginger Gregson and Lori User walked behind us.

"Hey, Jamie, you still goin' over to Toothpick's house every night?" he asked loudly, with a sly glance in Ginger's direction.

"Yeah, every night, Beave," I said even louder and added in a serious tone, "You know, we make love, smoke dope, and push needles into voodoo dolls."

Before he could get another word out, I said in a menacing voice, "In fact, Janice is workin' on a doll that looks just like you!"

Old Beaver turned about twelve shades of red while Harvey, Lori, and Ginger laughed like crazy.

Before I'd only been able to come up with a cool response to somebody's putdown when I was sitting by myself at home or riding alone on the school bus, but now I tried to say whatever popped into my brain. It didn't always work, but I was trying to change.

I used to worry how bad things might turn out. You know—what if I flunk geometry, what if I rip my jockstrap in gym, what if Balkler makes us read our literature biographies out loud and I throw up or something. I could go on and on. But Janice kept reminding me, "Don't worry, Jamie, just be you. OK?" And that's what I tried to be: just me.

I even started doing some crazy things I'd never had the guts to do before. I went over to Weird Creatures, the local aquarium shop, and bought something I'd always wanted: a tarantula. I know most people freak out when they see spiders, but they don't bother me—although I'll admit that snakes give me the creeps. One day I brought home this really cool-looking red and brown Mexican tarantula; I named him Fremont.

My parents weren't exactly thrilled. In fact, my mom said she'd never clean my room again. Promises, promises! But I really dig tarantulas, and Fremont was there to stay.

I don't know if you are aware of it, but a tarantula sheds its skin much like a snake, and what's left over is a pretty good replica of the spider. So one day I came a little early to Introduction to Great Literature and did something absolutely crazy. Something that shy, mousy Jamie Almont wouldn't have done before. When Miss Balkler came strolling in with a book after the bell rang, she saw Fremont's skin lying on top of her desk—right next to her box of pink facial tissues. I thought she might have a stroke or something, but instead she gritted her teeth, made a loud karate shout, and crushed the spider skin with *The Collected Works of Shakespeare*, Volume I. It really freaked us out; I don't think that class had ever been so awake.

Another thing I began to do was talk to girls; I don't mean the usual "Hi!" or "How ya doin'?" I actually started a few genuine conversations with my female classmates—even Ginger. *That* was really an accomplishment.

One day riding home in the bus, Harvey was bragging about the new pool his dad was going to have installed in the summer. I got the idea we should have a neighborhood swim party, which would naturally include Ginger.

"You gonna ask her?" Harv said, half believing me.

"Yeah," I said positively. I began trying to think of something slick to say, when it hit me.

"Hey, Ginger," I announced, leaning back over a bus seat to face her and June Larson sitting together. "Whattaya say to coming over to a swim party at Harvey's as soon as he gets his new pool put in? You, too, June."

Ginger gave me one of those "Are you kiddin'?" looks until I said, "Listen, Ginger, you'll break poor old Mr. Brenhouser's heart if you don't come."

She really cracked up then, and so did Harv. See, last July Harvey and I were riding home with his dad in the family station wagon when we saw Ginger bicycling toward us. No matter how she's dressed, Ginger is a real eye-grabber, but on this hot day she was wearing an orange bikini. Well, Mr. Brenhouser nearly ran over a mailbox while he was gawking at Ginger.

"Good night, nurse!" he shouted. "That girl's a hazard to traffic!" Harv and I laughed so hard tears rolled down our cheeks.

Ginger remembered us going haywire in the car, and

then Harvey filled her in on all the details when school began.

"I guess you'll want me to wear my bikini, huh?" She laughed.

"But of course," I replied with a wink.

"Man, are you smokin' dope or what?" Harvey asked me as we walked away from the bus stop.

"Come on, Jamie," Rick razzed, "you used to pee in your pants if Ginger even came near you. Now you're inviting her to wear her bikini over to Harvey's so his dad can drool over her."

"What's the matter?" I said. "You got something against drool?"

It wasn't like I had nerves of steel or anything; I just tried not to let people, or things they said, get to me like before. I guess I didn't realize at the time that when you change—even if it's for the good—sometimes there's a price to pay. It started with small things, but then it worked itself up into a real blowout later on.

Pretty soon I wasn't always sitting next to Harvey or Rick on the school bus. Occasionally I sat down next to Janice, although that wasn't often because, as usual, she was absent a lot.

Once I sat down beside Ginger, and we had a genuine conversation together. I couldn't believe it. When I wasn't so hung up on myself and really concentrated on listening to the other person, people opened up and were friendly. Like Ginger, when I told her I just bought Michael Jackson's new duet with Streisand, she confessed she listened to a lot of her mom's old records besides the latest. You know, groups with names like the Four Seasons, the Drifters, the Beach Boys. . . .

"The Beach Boys!" I blurted out. "You mean 'I Get Around' and 'California Girls' Beach Boys?"

"Yeah!" she said enthusiastically. Then she kind of lowered her voice: "You know, I really *love* some of those old songs."

"Like 'Fun, Fun, Fun,' 'Sloop John B'?" I asked.

"Yes! Yes!" she practically squealed.

"I thought *I* was the only Beach Boys freak in our school!"

Well, in a matter of minutes Ginger and I agreed we listened to some of those old rock and rock groups almost as much as Michael Jackson, Boy George, or even Madonna's new album.

We also found out we both had aquariums, although Ginger definitely did not dig tarantulas.

"You mean you were the one who set up that prank in Balkler's room?" she whispered.

I nodded. The whole school knew the story, although Harv and Beaver had spiced it up a bit, saying that a live spider was about to crawl up Old Lady Balkler's hand before she clobbered him, and that a tarantula's bite can kill in fifteen seconds. Not true. Maybe its looks could kill, but a tarantula isn't poisonous.

Ginger seemed to be eyeing me with a lot more than just casual interest when we finished the ride home. As the bus rolled to our stop, she said with a smile, "Hey, maybe we should get together with our Beach Boys albums sometime. You know, sort of an unofficial fan club."

"Sure," I replied, almost losing my ability to speak and

my newfound self-confidence in one ecstatic moment. *Unreal!* I thought; Ginger Gregson inviting *me* to get together with *her*. Definitely an improvement since writing sick love notes in the ninth grade.

"Hey, what gives, Jamie?" Rick asked as we walked along the road to our homes. The Beaver was an accomplished eavesdropper and had obviously picked up my conversation with Ginger.

"First Toothpick gets the hots for you, and now even Ginger thinks you're worth looking at. I don't get it," the Beaver concluded.

I have to admit I was almost gloating, but I tried not to rub it in.

"I don't know, Rick," I said casually. "Things just seem to be going differently now, that's all. Who knows?" I laughed. "Maybe it's my new aftershave."

"Yeah?" Harv asked seriously. "What kind are you using?"

"Come on, Harv," Beaver whined. "No aftershave is gonna help *you!*"

"What's that supposed to mean?" Harvey growled.

Beaver and I both looked at Harvey and laughed. I think Harv had been wearing the same shirt for over a week; I could still see the chili stain he'd gotten on his collar three days ago.

"Harv," I tried to say as kindly as possible, "sometimes just a more frequent change in wardrobe might help." But he only stared back at me with a mixture of confusion and irritation.

"Harvey isn't gonna change for anybody, Jamie, you know that," Rick said matter-of-factly. "He just dresses . . . well, sort of comfortably, that's all." But you couldn't miss the putdown Beaver tried to hide between the lines.

It's hard to be tactful with Harvey; sometimes you feel like saying, "Hey, Harv, when you smell like a water buffalo and part of last week's lunch is still hanging on your shirt, it's a real turn-off. You know what I mean?" But I didn't want that to be my scene anymore.

I went right home that day. Luckily, the three of us couldn't get together because Harv had an appointment with the dentist for some fillings. I guess Harv doesn't practice much dental hygiene either.

So instead I took Benny for a walk out in some fields that used to be a farm but "soon will become magically transformed"—that's what the sign said anyway—into a country village. There's plenty of space for old Benny to run, and it gave me some time to think.

Have you ever wanted something for so long that when it finally comes true you go into shock? I mean that's how I felt about my newly budding friendship with Ginger. *Now* what was I supposed to do? Sure, she said let's get together, but it just seemed like things were moving too fast. And what bothered me, too, was not being able to talk about it with Harvey or Rick. They seemed a lot more envious than enthused about my success and confidence.

When Benny and I got back to the house and I started to brush the dirt off of us—Mom isn't thrilled with muddy paw prints on the white living room carpet—it hit me: the person I really wanted to talk to was Toothpick. She'd been absent for a couple of days again, so I thought I would call and ask how she was doing. I suppose I really wanted to talk about my problem, but at least the conversation wasn't going to start off that way.

My mother was watching *Our Daily Bread*, that new religious soap opera, on her portable in the sewing room, so I knew she couldn't zero in on our conversation.

After I dialed the number, a real raspy voice at the other end answered, "Hello?"

"Hello, Janice?" I asked, not sure it was her.

"Jamie? Hi, how are you?" came a husky reply, followed by a lot of coughing.

"How are *you*?" I asked.

"Lots better today, thanks."

"You got the flu or something?" I asked, forgetting for a moment about that strange illness she had.

She chuckled a little, then coughed some more. "No, it's just that problem I told you about, acting up and giving me a hard time."

I surprised myself when I blurted out, "It's really good to hear your voice."

"That's the nicest thing you've ever said to me, Jamie," she said quickly. "That sort of makes my day."

When she said that, I wondered if I was getting in too deep—you know. I truly wanted her as a friend, and I *was* concerned, but I didn't want her to think I was getting the hots for her. There was a long pause, and then she asked right out of the blue, "Have you made a hit with Ginger yet?"

It freaked me out. "Have you got ESP or what?" I asked. I was glad she brought up the subject, but it blew me away that she seemed to know what had happened.

"I knew you'd talk to her someday, and that if you'd let the real you shine through, she'd be impressed," Janice explained.

"You're something," I said with admiration.

"So are you," she replied and then began to cough again. When the coughing finally stopped, she asked excitedly, "Well, aren't you going to tell me what happened?"

When I explained about the bus ride home and how Ginger and I had realized we really grooved on old Beach Boys albums, Janice laughed. "The Beach Boys! I can't stand them, but everybody has their own tastes." I also told her how Ginger sort of invited me over.

"Sounds like you have a new friend," Janice said after I gave her all the details.

"Yeah, I suppose," I replied, not sounding too positive. Janice picked up on that right away.

"The next move is yours, Jamie," she said quietly and matter-of-factly.

"What do you mean?" I asked.

"She isn't going to come swooping down on you. If she did, she'd probably scare you away. *You* have to follow through. . . . Do something crazy," she explained.

"Like what? I mean, Janice, I start shaking just thinking about asking her out."

"When you put that tarantula skin on Balkler's desk, you did it because you wanted to. Jamie, use your imagination."

"You mean like I should put a scorpion on her lunch tray?" I said in a deranged whisper.

Janice laughed, then coughed some more after I said that. "Now you're talking!"

"OK, Janice. I'll be myself, I guess. And just do whatever my weird mind comes up with."

CHAPTER 7

Except for the bus rides and sometimes running into each other in the cafeteria, I saw Ginger in only one of my classes during the day—Modern European History with Mr. Kellog. Kellog is probably my favorite teacher; he has a weird sense of humor, and being sort of weird myself, I guess that's why I like him.

Once when he was busy showing us pictures of the present-day leaders of Europe on the overhead projector—like who cares?—someone stuck the Playmate of the Month into his stack of photos.

After a grainy black-and-white shot of the prime minister of Czechoslovakia, out flashes a full-color portrait of Miss February! Everyone gasped and waited for Kellog to freak out or something, but he never missed a beat.

"Ah! I hoped I'd brought this along. This is Sweden's Elvira Goodboden, an eccentric head of state who demands that everything be out in the open during cabinet meetings."

While everyone cracked up, Kellog went on with the rest of his lecture, just like the Playmate was supposed to be there.

So two days after Ginger and I realized we both liked the Beach Boys, I waltzed into Kellog's class with a poster made from a Beach Boys album cover. "Mr. Kellog," I announced, "I have a group portrait I'd like you to put up on the Current World Leaders bulletin board."

The kids standing around us started laughing, and good old Kellog went into another of his corny routines.

"Well, now, this is a real find! Where did you get this, Almont? Most of you realize, of course, that this is a rare early photograph of Men at Work when they were simply known as the 'Washed on the Beach' Boys."

Ginger was impressed when she saw the picture, and naturally it gave me a chance to ask her, "What do you think?"

"I love it!"

"Do you think you could find a place for it on a wall in your room?" This was my way of giving it to her, I just couldn't walk up and say, "Here!" I hoped Ginger would take it home in a few weeks, when Kellog emptied the bulletin board.

Right then she gave me a sweet smile and said sexily, "I know just the place."

I don't think I heard a word from Kellog or anybody else the rest of that class. All I could picture was Ginger inviting me over to her house to listen to some old Beach Boys records and admiring their portrait in her room.

I finally started to come down from the clouds last hour during Art and Music Appreciation. I kept waiting for Janice to come in—we had started sitting together in the class for a while—and I wanted to tell her what had happened. But the bell rang, Mr. Pitts started to show us these weird-looking paintings of fat naked ladies by some guy named Picasso, and still no Janice. This was strange, because even though she hadn't come to school on the bus, I saw her in the hall after math class and figured she had checked in late or something.

She wasn't on the bus going home either, and after I promised Harv I'd meet him at his house later, I trotted home to call her. It was one of those damp, dreary sort of days Michigan is famous for—the kind when people get the blahs or fall sick—but it didn't bother me. Things were going too well for me to complain about crumby spring weather.

We'd just gotten one of those new cordless phones with an automatic-redial button, so I took it into my room, turned on the Stooges, and kept trying again and again during the commercials. I cradled the phone between my ear and shoulder while I sprinkled some food in my aquarium. I noticed one of my black-laced angelfish barely nibbling at the flakes as they sank in the water. Black-laced angels are beautiful but not very hardy; it looked like this one might die.

I also gave good old Fremont, his red and brown tarantula fur glistening with good health, a green cricket to munch on. Eating is about the only thing that makes him move around; the rest of the time he's motionless. I think tarantulas must be deep thinkers or something.

Mrs. Brooks answered at about the ninth try. After I asked to speak to Janice, her mother replied in a troubled voice, "I'm afraid Janice can't come to the phone, Jamie."

I was worried. "Is she all right, Mrs. Brooks?" There was a long pause. Janice's mom was definitely having a hard time coming up with an explanation.

"Jamie, Janice is in the hospital," she blurted out.

"The hospital?" I interrupted.

She explained hesitantly, "Janice tries to lead as normal a life as she can. But it's not easy to do with cystic fibrosis."

For a moment I couldn't speak, but finally I said, "Janice told me about it. Could you spell that for me, Mrs. Brooks?"

She spelled the two words slowly. A little shaken, I grabbed a pencil from my desk and wrote it down carefully on the Three Stooges poster hanging on my closet door.

"I know Janice will be delighted you called, Jamie. As soon as she can take calls in her room, maybe you could talk to her."

"Do you know when that will be?"

"We hope by tomorrow evening. She's only going through her usual treatment. She doesn't have a serious infection at this time, so don't worry. Call me tomorrow night, Jamie. All right?"

"OK, Mrs. Brooks."

Cystic fibrosis. I walked into the living room and picked out Volume C of the encyclopedia off Mom's well-dusted shelves. Now that Janice was in the hospital, I wanted to find out more about her condition. Preferring the sounds of my aquarium to the ticking of the living room grandfather clock—it always reminded me of a funeral home—I returned to my room and looked up cystic fibrosis.

It was like looking at the first page of last year's final biology exam. You sort of go into shock with all the big words: "a hereditary disease in which the lungs, liver, and pancreas are affected... difficulty breathing, cannot digest food properly... many die of lung infections... cannot be cured."

"Cannot be cured," I said softly to myself. I thought of last year when I was out of school for a week with strep throat. It seemed like I'd never get well those seven days at home; the only time I'd ever been to a hospital was to visit my grandmother after she'd had a heart attack.

Janice was in the hospital for her "usual treatment," her mother said. I thought how she coughed a lot, took those funny-looking pills whenever she ate, and still kept smiling.

At first I really got down on myself. You know, all those times talking about me and my problems, and only once did I ask her what was wrong, why she looked or sounded bad.

It was time to take Benny for a long walk. Suddenly things were all screwed up in my mind. I felt like I was half dressed in the locker room during a fire drill in November. Man, give me a break!

When I got back from walking my dog, I felt a little more sane. I walked in the door and my mom said, "You got two phone calls while you were out, Jamie."

Harvey had called, I supposed, wondering where I was, but my mother added with a wink, "The last one left her number and asked you to call back."

"Janice?" I said anxiously.

My mother gave me a quizzical look before saying, "No, she said her name was Ginger."

CHAPTER 8

"You mean Ginger actually called *you?*" Harvey asked for about the third time.

"Yeah," I mumbled.

Harv and I sat alone in his rec room at one of the game tables, but no game was being played.

"And you haven't called her back?" he continued.

"No. I guess I can't get into it."

"Listen," Harvey offered, "maybe if you call her from here, you won't be so nervous. And I could listen in on one of the extensions to see if you screw up or anything," he added hopefully.

"Thanks, Harv," I replied. "You're a real pal. That's not it, anyway. I'm not nervous about callin' Ginger."

"Hey, I'm only tryin' to help! What's the big deal?"

I felt miserable. I didn't think Harv would understand. I barely understood myself.

"It's got something to do with Janice," I said finally.

"Who?"

"Come on, Harv. Toothpick!" I said angrily.

Harvey's forehead wrinkled in confusion. Finally, he asked, "Do you like her or something?"

I gave a long sigh. "She's been a good friend, Harv. And she's sick, really sick. She's got a disease called cystic fibrosis but doesn't want anyone to know. I've been leaning on her and learning from her ever since we met. And I don't think I've ever asked her what she feels about anything."

"Cystic... thrombosis?" Harv asked.

I shook my head. "Fibrosis. Cystic *fibrosis*. It's a respiratory disease. People who have it usually don't live longer than eighteen."

A look of concern appeared in Harvey's eyes. "Sounds bad," he said.

"She's the one who psyched me up to make a move with Ginger," I continued. "She's really helped me out. And now things are going like I'd always dreamed they would. Ginger calls me, for crying out loud! But I can't call her back because... because I want Janice to know I care about her. Does any of that make sense?"

Harvey sat silently for a moment before blurting out, "Sure. Hey, I know what you can do. Send Toothpick—I mean Janice—some flowers. Then you're off the hook. You don't hafta feel guilty no more. You showed her you care. Then"—he paused—"call up Ginger, man! Before you screw things up with her."

I know Harvey's solution was pretty simple, and it brushed off my feelings about Janice. But in the end that's what I did: flowers for Janice and then a phone call to Ginger.

"We have a nice 'pick me up' bouquet that is very popular," the florist girl with severe sinus problems described over the phone.

"Ah . . . how much is it?" I asked meekly.

"Fifteen ninety-eight plus tax," came the curt reply. After Harvey saw me freeze and turn white, he ran to the other extension and blurted out, "Could you tell us what your cheapest flowers cost?" Harv has a real way with words.

"We can send a single white carnation in a long-stemmed vase for three ninety-five," she snapped.

I ran quickly to the other room and nodded to Harv and he took care of the rest of the details.

"Now that we got that settled, it's time to call Ginger," he said with obvious relish. For poor Harv, listening in on a phone call to Ginger would be almost as good as making it himself.

"You don't think the flower is too much?" I asked.

"What? One lousy carnation? Listen, girls love that stuff! She'll probably cry or somethin' and say, 'Oh, that's so sweet.' I mean what else can you do, man? That's really being friendly. Now . . . call Ginger!"

Somehow I thought Janice would get the message that I cared. If not with the flower, then some other way.

"Let's do it," I finally said.

"I'll dial for ya," Harv offered, "and then duck into my dad's office and listen from there. Hey, what's the number?"

"I don't know."

Harvey rolled his eyes and said, "Hold it. I'll be right back." He raced upstairs.

In about thirty seconds he was back with a little black

address book. Harvey Brenhouser, who'd never been on a date in his life, who was nearly as afraid of girls as I was, had a little black book filled with the phone numbers and addresses of about fifty girls. It read like the "Top Forty Bods" of Glenwood High School.

"Harvey"—I started laughing—"some of these girls have already graduated!"

"So?" he replied. "You never know when it might come in handy. Like now!"

I found Ginger's number, and Harv flashed to his father's extension.

Ginger's unmistakable sexy voice answered, "Hello?"

"Hi, Ginger," I began. "This is Stan LeBan the Tarantula Man. Did you call me?" No, I couldn't say, "It's me, Jamie." I thought I better use some humor to disguise my nervousness.

She cracked up. After she stopped laughing she asked, "Is that you, Jamie?"

"Yeah, how ya doin'?" I replied.

"Fine. I wanted to know if you felt like helping me with Kellog's homework assignment?"

"Ah, sure." I said tentatively. Ginger had an A average in everything. Still, you need some excuse, right?

"Later on, we can groove on the Beach Boys."

"Sounds great!" I said with genuine enthusiasm.

After I told her I'd be right over after supper, we ended the conversation.

I heard Harv yell from his father's office, "Man! I still can't believe it! Ginger calls Jamie up and invites him over!" I didn't know if he was telling his mom, his sister Freda, or maybe the wall. But it sure felt good.

I hoped Janice liked the flower.

Ginger Gregson lives in a really plush house in the middle of our subdivision. After supper, I told my folks I was off to do some homework at a friend's. That's what I usually said whenever I was going to see Janice, so they assumed I'd be studying with her, not Ginger.

"You mean at your girlfriend's?" my father teased.

"Well, you never know, Dad," I replied with a grin. That sort of caught him off guard. I usually try to mutter unintelligibly when he discusses Janice.

Ginger introduced me to her mother when I first arrived. Her mom looked like she was dressed for a night on the town, but when I checked out the museum-type furniture, I thought maybe that's why she dressed that way. All the chairs looked like the kind of stuff you look at—not sit on. Ginger's dad was working late on a legal case or something. I'm not sure what he does, but he gets a lot of dough for it.

Ginger looked gorgeous in Levis and a pullover sweater. We walked upstairs to her room to do our homework.

Her room was about twice the size of mine. We plopped down on the floor in front of this massive stereo system and spread our homework in front of us. I don't know if it was her perfume or powder, but it sure smelled good in there. I suddenly realized I'd never been in a girl's room before.

As we sat next to each other, Ginger started explaining how she had done Kellog's assignment, and I really studied her face close-up for the first time. You know, a beautiful person kind of loses a little sparkle up close like that. I'd always pictured Ginger as being perfect, but now that little mole on her left cheek didn't look like a beauty mark anymore, and I noticed one of her teeth was crooked.

"What are you looking at, Jamie?" she asked with a smile.

"At you. You're pretty," I answered.

"You're sweet." She giggled.

The romantics over, we whipped through our homework on Western Europe's contribution to NATO's defense. Ginger had brains *and* beauty. I ended up copying most of her answers.

When the schoolwork was finished, Ginger grabbed one of her old Beach Boys albums and we listened together. Ginger even tried to teach me how to sing harmony—she's in Girl's Choir—and I soon had her in stitches with my attempts to sing the high notes on "Good Vibrations."

I had no difficulty getting her to laugh, and I guess that was my biggest attraction for her. It certainly wasn't my manly physique. Then I remembered what Janice had said about Ginger's true opinion of Joe Pentatella, and I thought maybe macho hunks weren't the only guys she was interested in.

"Ginger, have you ever heard of cystic fibrosis?" I asked suddenly as she put the third album we'd listened to into its record sleeve.

"No," she replied seriously. "Is that something you're studying in biology?"

"No, I don't have biology. But a friend of mine has it. Cystic fibrosis, I mean. It's a disease, I guess."

"Sounds awful. Like some kind of cancer."

"No, it's not. But it might as well be," I replied grimly.

"Is it someone at school?" she asked.

"I guess I'd better not say right now," I said slowly, studying the design of Ginger's bedroom carpet. "I don't know if they want a lot of people to know about it."

"I understand," she said, and I knew she did. "You know, for someone with such a crazy sense of humor, you're really sensitive to people."

"I am?"

"I think so." She laughed.

When it was time to head for home, Ginger walked me to the door. "The student council decided last night to hold a Sadie Hawkins Dance two weeks from now," Ginger said as I put on my jacket.

"What's a Sadie Hawkins Dance?" I asked.

"It's sort of a hillbilly thing. Everyone dresses like farmers with bibbed overalls." Then she added with a smile, "It's also a role reversal—the girls ask the boys to the dance."

"Oh yeah?" I replied.

After a slight pause, she asked softly, "Wanna go?"

"You . . . and me?" I asked.

"Yeah, you and me." She smiled.

"OK . . . I mean, yeah! Of course!" I finally stammered.

I guess you could say I was a little spaced out after my evening with Ginger. I walked halfway down our street before I realized I had passed my own house.

CHAPTER 9

Last night's glow still showed on my face the following morning. When I got to the bus stop everyone was grumbling about the drizzle falling on us while we waited, but I was all smiles, happy with the world.

I knew Harv must have filled in the Beaver on the latest events. In fact, when I got back from Ginger's, there was an urgent message that Harvey had called and I should call him back. I didn't, though. I wanted to enjoy the ecstasy I was in a little longer. I figured Harv could wait and hear all the details tomorrow.

As Harv and Rick gave me the once-over, I guess the look on my face told them it was *too* good to hear about. Oh well, what are friends for? All Harvey managed to say before the bus arrived was, "How can you be smilin' on such a pukey day?"

I knew they wanted to know the details but just couldn't ask, so I decided to let the suspense build a little. Later in the day, when the three of us passed Ginger in the hall, she said, "Hi, Jamie. That was fun last night. Hey, do you think you can find some bibbed overalls?"

"I'm workin' on it." I smiled.

That was too much for Harvey. As Ginger walked away, he grabbed my arm and pleaded, "Well, you gonna tell us or what?"

They walked in silence down the hall as I described my visit to Ginger's and her inviting me to the girl-ask-boy dance.

After giving them the latest, we walked on in silence a few moments longer. I guess the news had to slowly soak through brain tissue.

"You mean she asked you to go to the dance?" Harvey cried.

"Yeah. Isn't that a kick?" I replied.

I was happy with life, but it was beginning to bother me that Rick and Harv still didn't seem overjoyed with my budding romance. And the Beaver lost no time in trying to think of something to put a damper on things.

"You know," he began slowly, "it just occurred to me why Ginger is asking you to that dance."

Rick always sees ulterior motives for anything anyone does. I guess it's because he has so many ulterior motives himself.

"What?" Harv asked.

"Ginger's been dating Joe for how long? Ever since last year, right? So lately Joe hasn't been the perfect Romeo, and Ginger's gonna liven things up a bit."

"You mean she's trying to make Joe Pentatella jealous by

asking Jamie to the dance?" Harv asked doubtfully.

"What else?" the Beaver replied.

I laughed a bit and said, "So Joe goes into a rage, beats the snot out of me for foolin' around with his girl, and he and Ginger live happily ever after?"

"Aw, come on, you know what I mean," Rick continued weakly.

"Yeah? I don't know what you mean." Harvey chuckled.

Later in the day, still not sure, Harvey went up to Joe and struck up a conversation about the dance since a lot of student council members were putting up signs to advertise the coming event. When Joe didn't give any hints as to whether he expected Ginger to ask him, Harvey asked him point blank. That's when we learned old Joe had the hots for Vicki Pembler, a knock-out redhead who had transferred here after Christmas vacation. Evidently Joe thought Vicki's red hair—and, ah, other physical attractions—were a real turn-on. So the Beaver's theory sort of went down the toilet.

While Harvey and Rick tried to figure out what Ginger saw in me, my feelings about Janice came back to haunt me suddenly during math.

While we were working on some problems, Mr. Gomez got a request from the office to send homework for an extended length of time. It didn't even occur to me who they were referring to until Gomez asked, "How long do they expect her to be out?" Then I knew—Janice.

No one asked or remembered about Toothpick's being gone. After coming up with the flower idea, even Harvey hadn't mentioned her. Like nobody cared.

Later, when everyone stampeded to the cafeteria, I

started to make my way in the opposite direction.

"Hey, where ya goin'?" Harv yelled from the crowd.

"Gotta make a phone call," I replied, flattening myself against the wall so I wouldn't be crushed by a mob just out of the auto shop.

According to the walls of the booth I was in, various sexual services could be arranged by dialing any of several numbers scratched into the wall's peeling green paint. One of the numbers was Ginger's. I guess that's the price you pay for popularity. People suggest you do some unmentionable things.

I dialed Janice's home phone, hoping to catch Mrs. Brooks and get the number at the hospital.

Janice's mother answered after the third ring. She seemed happy to hear my voice and said Janice would want to hear from me. Pretty soon a new phone number was scratched onto the wall. Although this one was to room 616, St. Joseph's Hospital.

When Janice answered, she sounded a lot better than I expected.

"Is that you, Jamie?" she asked.

"Yeah. How are you feeling?" I asked. I realized this was one time I asked and really wanted to know.

"Better. Lots better, in fact. Jamie . . . I got your flower just a little while ago."

"Yeah," I mumbled.

"That was really sweet. Did you know carnations are my favorite flowers?"

"Uh-uh," I replied. I thought all girls were supposed to be crazy about roses.

"Thanks again. It was really pretty," she said.

There was a long pause, and I guess she could hear all the noise coming from the hallway—locker doors slamming, kids yelling, and stuff.

"It sounds like you're in the middle of a riot at school." She laughed.

"Yeah," I said again. I'm a great phone conversationalist!

"Why didn't you wait till you got home. Won't you miss lunch or something?" she asked.

And then it hit me. Why had I called now? And I told her. "I was worried! Gee, all of a sudden you were in the hospital, and I didn't know why. I guess I just wanted to hear your voice and make sure you're all right."

"That's the best thing I've heard for days!" she said. "But hey, I'm sorry I didn't tell you before. I mean about going to the hospital. I guess my mom gave you the word."

"Yeah," I said, starting to feel a little uncomfortable.

"I know that wasn't fair—not telling you, I mean. But a lot of people learn about cystic fibrosis and say, 'Oh, no, like cancer, huh?,' and I'd just rather not have people see me that way."

"I don't see it that way," I protested. "You're my friend, and when you're ill, then I wanna help. I mean, as much as I can."

I heard her sigh. "You've helped a lot already. You're so open about your feelings; I was the one holding back—thinking you might be turned off by hearing every detail about my stupid disease."

"I'm your friend, Janice. No matter what, OK?"

"OK. Jamie . . . thanks for calling," she said softly. "Hey"—

she laughed—"You'd better get to lunch or you'll miss out on all the good food!"

"Yeah." I laughed in return. "I'll see you later."

We said good-bye, and I walked slowly down the hall to get in the lunch line, the fragrant aroma of tator tots, fish sandwiches, and cafeteria hot dogs wafting my way.

Being one of the last in line, I got to choose among the assorted delicacies left beyind by everyone else. After finding a sandwich and Jell-O salad that didn't look like they would cause immediate death, I scanned the crowd for Rick and Harvey. But someone nearby was waving at me, and I moved in that direction. It was Ginger.

She was sitting at one of the few round tables in the cafeteria, and right next to her sat the Hump. That struck me as a bit odd, because Jerome usually sits at the table occupied by the school jocks.

"Wanna join us?" Ginger asked, smiling up at me.

"Thanks," I replied, stumbling into a chair across from her. I guess my conversation with Janice and now an unexpected luncheon with Ginger and the Hump sort of put me off balance.

I had obviously interrupted the Hump's conversation because he gave me a fish-eyed stare and continued, "Like I was saying, Ginger, this girl-ask-boy stuff is kind of new to me."

"Oh, Jerry, we had a Sadie Hawkins Dance the first year we were here," she replied. "Anyway, I'm sure someone will be asking you," she continued.

While I cautiously tasted my sandwich, hoping it would be edible, the Hump went on. "Then why fight temptation?

Here I am now—and available!" He put his arm around Ginger. "Why take any chances by being asked by someone else?" I'll say one thing for the Hump—he's not lacking in self-confidence. One of his favorite sayings is "Last year I was conceited, but this year I'm perfect."

"I guess you'll have to take that chance," Ginger said with a smile. "You see, I've already asked someone else."

Did that embarrass the Hump? No way. "Well, you can't say I didn't give you the opportunity," he concluded. "See ya around." He left the table, never once acknowledging my presence.

"I wonder if Jerome will ever realize he's not God's gift to women." Ginger sighed, watching him stride to another table of eligible beauties. As I sat there eating in silence, she looked my way. "Real talkative today, huh?"

"I'm just a careful eater. I don't wanna die young from an overripe fish sandwich."

Ginger laughed. "It's pretty bad, isn't it?"

We sat in silence for a few moments longer before Ginger asked, "Thinking about your sick friend?"

I looked at her in amazement. "Does it show on my face or something?"

"No," she answered, "just a lucky guess, I suppose. Any news?"

"She's doing better," I said enthusiastically. "In fact, I talked to her on the phone just before I came down here."

"That's good." She smiled, slightly nodding her head.

After we finished eating lunch, Ginger asked me to walk her to biology. I felt comfortable with just the two of us together. It was only when someone else joined us that I clammed up.

By the time we got to the bio lab on the second floor, we were walking alone, and I whispered, "Ginger, I have a terrible confession to make." She gave me a questioning look. Then I continued, "You've asked me to a dance less than two weeks from now, and I don't know how to dance!"

Ginger burst out laughing so loud that several people turned our way.

"Don't laugh!" I whispered like Count Dracula. "It makes me very angry!"

When she stopped laughing, she gently took hold of my arm and said, "Listen, we'll just have to have some dance lessons before then."

"You mean we're gonna dance to old Beach Boys albums?"

"No"—she giggled— "we'll get down and boogie to the latest. Don't worry, I'm a good teacher."

"Sounds fine to me," I said.

I didn't see Ginger on the bus going home that afternoon. She was probably at another student council meeting.

Harvey and I sat in a seat together, staring out the window. It had been thundering loudly, and everybody was scrambling to get on board their buses.

All of a sudden Harvey started laughing, still staring out the window. "What's the deal?" I asked.

"You should see Rick. What a fool!" Sometimes Harv will start laughing like that for no reason, which sort of gives me the creeps, but this time he offered an explanation.

"I think Rick just found out that Tracy Haynes ain't gonna ask him to that dance."

All of a sudden a drenching rain came pouring down, and the Beaver jumped on board the bus looking like he'd just been hosed down. He had a forlorn look on his face. He must've been counting on Tracy.

"Come on, Beaver! Hurry it up!" came a familiar cry from the bus door. The last few stragglers included the Hump, who was really soaked. Apparently his limousine wasn't running, and he was forced to ride the bus.

As the bus jerked and rolled out of the parking lot, and Rick found a seat across the aisle from us, Harv started cackling again, slapping his hands on his knees for dramatic effect.

"Aw, shut up, Brenhouser," Rick uttered miserably.

"Aw-w-w, whatsa matter? Did little Ricky get shot down by Tracy?" Harvey teased.

Then all of a sudden the Beaver smiled at Harv's antics and said, "Yeah, the little snot. Who wants to go to some goofy dance with her anyway?"

"You did," Harvey said knowingly, to which Rick offered no reply.

"I know somebody who got asked to the dance already," the Beaver announced with a sly grin.

"Well, don't keep us in suspense, Beave. Who, pray tell, is this fortunate fellow?" the Hump asked sarcastically.

"Jamie," Rick announced, with the drama he usually saves for a juicy piece of gossip, "got asked by Ginger."

The Hump blinked a couple of times. "Jamie *who?*" he inquired.

Harv started to laugh again, and the Beaver's grin got even wider when he said, "Jamie Almont."

"You mean the Jamie Almont who lives in our subdivision?" the Hump asked in a shocked voice, though he was looking right at me.

"Yep!"

"You mean *that* Jamie Almont?" he said, pointing at me in disgust.

By this time Harv, Rick, and a few others sitting around us were cracking up.

"Oh well, I guess wonders never cease." The Hump sighed and then turned his attention elsewhere.

For the first time in a long while I wasn't able to offer a good response to such a putdown. In fact, I was feeling pretty confused and inadequate. I guess there was something missing—Janice. Before, I had really thrived on the confidence she gave me. Now things were kind of murky.

The Hump gave one last word of wisdom as we got off the bus. "You know, James, I thought that Toothpick was your chicky-poo, and now you're trying to make a move on Ginger. You're gonna mess things up."

It continued raining as we trudged down the streets, and there wasn't much conversation. I was glad of that.

CHAPTER 10

You're gonna mess things up. The Hump's words kept tumbling through my mind like gym shorts in a drier.

On the surface things looked great. I had overcome the awesome obstacle of getting close to Ginger, my dream girl. It even seemed like things were going in the right direction. We liked each other, and I was beginning to relax and enjoy being with her—not throwing up or breaking out in a rash. It had all been due to Janice's helping me out. When I thought about that for a while, I knew what I wanted to do.

It didn't take long to sneak our new cordless phone out of the kitchen, where my mom was baking a pie, to my bedroom for a little privacy.

"Hi, Janice," I said when she answered the phone.

"Jamie?" she rasped.

"Yeah."

She started coughing real violently, and I was afraid something was terribly wrong, but finally she caught her breath.

"Sorry about that," she said a little more easily. "I just got back from treatment and everything's still . . . well, I won't bore you with details."

"Janice," I said, pausing a few moments again, "I miss you."

"I miss you, too," she said matter-of-factly. "This hospital routine is getting to be a drag. I wish I was home." She sighed.

"Could I come and see you?" I blurted out.

She hesitated a moment before saying, "Only immediate family are allowed on this floor, because of the oxygen and stuff. But you could say you were my brother!" she decided happily.

"What about your parents?"

"My mom can't make it tonight, and my dad has a bad cold. You're not allowed up here if you've got any upper respiratory problems—unless you're a patient, that is," she added.

There was no one else to see her that night. I knew she wanted me to visit if I could.

"I can't promise," I said, "but I think I can get a ride there. If I don't, I'll call you again later."

"OK!" she said.

After we said good-bye, I dialed Harvey's number. I didn't want to ask my dad for the car because I would have hard enough time talking him into letting me borrow it

for the dance with Ginger. I was hoping Harv would be up
for a little adventure.

"Hey, you wanna come over," he began after I said hello,
"and help me fix my brother's motorized dragon? You know
the one that really breathes smoke all over ya?"

"That sounds like fun, Harv, but listen: I was wondering
if you could borrow your mom's car and we could drive up
to St. Joseph's Hospital?"

"Are you kiddin', man?" Harvey whined. "I don't wanna—"

"Wait, Harv. Janice is really depressed, so I thought I'd
cheer her up." I went on to describe my plan. I could feel
the new Jamie returning again.

After Harv heard all the details, he cracked up. "You're
really gonna do that? Hey, let's ask Rick to come along,
this'll be great!"

"No, no," I replied, "they'll get suspicious with three
brothers. It better be just you and me."

Harvey had to honk the horn about twenty times in our
driveway before I could get out the door. My dad looked
up from his newspaper long enough to give me one of his
looks. "Is that guy mentally deranged or what?" looks.

"Harv and I are on a mission of mercy. I'll see ya," were
my parting words. Dad just crinkled his eyebrows a little
more in confusion—or maybe disgust.

"Do you have to lay on the horn like that whenever you
drive over here?" I greeted Harvey. "My dad thinks you
go crazy when you get behind the wheel."

"I do!" Harv laughed, his mouth full of Italian breadstick

There were crumbs already covering his dorky-looking air-
force jacket and the front seat of his mom's car.

"Want one?" he asked, pulling one from a bunch in his
top pocket and leaning my way. "They're my favorite—
garlic and onion!"

"Come on, Harv!" I cried after getting a full blast of his
breadstick breath. "They'll probably throw us out of the
hospital for polluting their air supply or something." Harvey
just laughed hysterically and pressed down harder on the
accelerator.

Although St. Joe's is normally a twenty-minute drive, we
got there in about eight flat. Besides munching on bread-
sticks, Harv likes to drive like a maniac.

I persuaded Harvey to leave his garlic-onion treats in
the car and got him to brush most of the crumbs off his
jacket before we reached the hospital lobby.

When we got to the reception desk, a hospital volun-
teer—you know, one of those blue-haired old ladies who
gives you the room passes—saw us, pressed her lips together in a frown, and asked, "Name, please?"

"Almont," I replied automatically.

While she typed out the name on her computer key-
board, Harv elbowed me and said, "Fool! Not you!"

"I mean Brooks, Janice Brooks," I corrected myself, feeling my face turning red under the old lady's glare.

A few moments later she snapped, "Janice Brooks is on
the sixth floor—Respiratory Diseases. Only immediate
family are allowed."

"She's my brother," I blurted out, and Harv immediately
groaned.

"Yes, I'm sure," the lady said with an icy smile. "But you'll have to obtain the passes on the sixth floor."

"This isn't gonna be easy," I whispered to Harvey as we walked to the elevators.

"You tellin' me? 'She's my brother!'" Harv laughed. "And they call *me* a nerd!"

"Shut up!" I whispered while others gathered around us in front of the elevators.

About a dozen people got on with us—it was really crowded—and we all started pressing buttons: 5, 4, 11, 9, 6. Everyone is so deathly quiet on an elevator. I was hoping Harvey could resist the temptation, but I was wrong. As we were going up, Harv said in a serious tone, "The doc said I got herpes, so we gotta burn all the furntiure."

Everybody kind of creeped over to the sides of the elevator, leaving us standing alone in the middle.

When we got off and the doors closed behind us, I couldn't help cracking up along with Harv even though I was ticked off, too.

"Brenhouser! You're gonna get us kicked out. And I wanna see Janice."

"Just tryin' to cheer people up," Harv said innocently. "They can feel better now, knowin' they ain't got it."

"Just shut up, OK?" I pleaded.

When we got to the nurses' station, we were both startled by the gorgeous nurse tending the cards. I mean, even in her uniform this girl made Miss January look like a slob.

While Harv and I stood there with our jaws hanging open, she asked, "Can I help you?"

"Ah . . . ah, yeah," I stammered. "I wanna see Janice

Brooks. . . . I'm her brother—Jamie Brooks."

"Brooks, Brooks," she whispered, as she thumbed through the cards. "Ah, here we are. Well, if you're her brother"— she looked up and smiled—"you know only immediate family are allowed. So I'm sorry your friend will have to stay behind."

"That's OK!" Harv said immediately. I knew with Ms. Gorgeous, R.N., to eyeball, he wouldn't mind waiting.

When I found Janice's room number, I sort of tiptoed into the room. It was semiprivate—you know, a curtain dividing the room in half for two patients. Janice was evidently next to the window, because the first person I saw was this old lady with an oxygen mask over her face. Her eyes sort of bugged out at me when I came in. There were oxygen tanks and all kinds of complicated stuff spread all over.

So my guts started knotting up because I half expected to see Janice with a mask over her face or tubes going up her nose, too, before I got around the partition.

But she was sitting up in bed reading and gave me the biggest smile when she saw me. "Hi!" she said happily. "So what brings you to this part of town?"

"Hi, Janice," I replied. I was really glad to see her. Even more than I thought I would be.

"It's nice to have company," she began. "I thought I'd have to sit through another hour of 'Family Feud' or some jerky game show." She pointed a thumb to the next bed and whispered, "My roommate's into that kind of stuff." The hospital TV, hanging from the wall, added an ugly pink glare to the room. Janice's roommate played the bedside control—first "Family Feud," then "The Muppet Show" and other assorted reruns.

"Oh well. You have me to stare at instead," I replied.

"Infinitely better."

I looked at her sitting in the bed as she put her book away. *Thin* wasn't the word for Janice. She looked so frail, it seemed she'd even lost weight since I last saw her at school.

She spotted the box I was carrying. I looked at it, too, explaining, "It's just a little surprise for later."

She smiled in response. "So what's the latest?" she demanded.

"What about you?" I answered. I was determined not to have our whole visit center on me.

Janice sighed. "It's always the same, Jamie. Maybe I'll be here another week or more. The weather doesn't help. I guess my lungs already have enough gunk without all the fog and dampness clogging things up. I just do the best I can," she said with a faraway look in her eyes.

There were some awkward moments of silence.

"Did you get in OK?" she asked.

"Yeah, it was a breeze," I answered.

"How's Ginger?" she asked with a flickering smile.

"Things are really great," I said, staring at the simple carnation I'd sent her; it was sitting on the little counter with her dinner tray. There were a couple of cards and a stuffed penguin, too.

"How great?" she asked.

"Ginger invited me to a dance coming up next week."

"Really? She asked you?" she said, grasping the little

vase the carnation was in and smiling at the flower. Then she looked up saying, "That *is* great."

"I miss you, though," I said slowly. "I miss the confidence you give me. And you know what? I miss your smile and your laugh, too."

"But you're doing pretty good on your own now," she said, glancing at the carnation again. "And I'm glad."

I sat there sort of speechless. I wanted to say something more, but she beat me to it.

"I liked what you said to me this morning," she began, taking my hand in hers. "I need a friend like you, someone who accepts *me* for what I am."

So I guess we were even then. We supported each other, but I still felt I was getting the better deal.

"Jamie," she whispered, "don't be cruel." I looked up, startled. "Would you please tell me what on earth is in that box?" She laughed.

I'd almost forgotten. "Well, I thought I'd try to cheer you up with an unexpected visitor." Then I added, "But you must be careful... you see, he *hates* hospitals."

"Sounds like my kind of person," she laughed, but obviously she knew who was in there.

"You keep that box off my bed, Almont, or I'll call a nurse," she joked.

"OK," I replied, gently lifting Fremont out of the watch box I'd brought him in. He seemed startled by all the bright overhead lights after being cooped up. He kept crawling nervously from one hand to the other.

"How can you stand that!" she squealed.

"He just feels like a big ball of fur, that's all," I explained.

"But he doesn't *look* like a ball of fur; he looks terrifying," she pointed out.

"Yeah, he seems like he's a bit nervous or something."

"Maybe you better put him back in the box," Janice suggested.

"Oh, he'll be all right in a minute. There. See, he just had to get use to the lights."

"You're a nut sometimes, you know," she said affectionately. Then she looked up at me. "Jamie, how could you ever worry about what people say? You hold that furry monster in your hands without batting an eyelash."

I shrugged. "I don't know. Maybe tarantulas hold the key to curing shyness."

Janice laughed. "Maybe."

Unfortunately, that was the end of our pleasant visit because just then in walked a nurse's aid wheeling a cart.

"Would you like some more ice water?" she began, but then saw Fremont sitting calmly on my knee near the bed. "A spider!" she screamed, and then tripped over one of the cart's rollers and threw half a pitcher of ice water on me and Fremont.

"A-ah-ah!" I yelled. The water hit me right in the lap. It didn't do Fremont much good either. He leaped off my knee and started racing for the door, like *fast*.

The startled nurse's aid jumped on top of Janice's bed screaming, "Get that thing out of here!" Meanwhile, Janice lay back in her bed, laughing hysterically.

I made for the door and grabbed a plastic cup to catch Fremont, yelling, "Hey, Harv, help me, would ya? Fremont's loose!"

Then a nurse walking toward Janice's room saw me and started to say, "What on earth—?" but just screamed and backed against the wall while she watched my red and brown tarantula tooling down the hall.

"I got him!" I yelled a minute later, scooping him up in the cup and covering it with my palm so he couldn't escape.

"What happened?" Harv cried when he reached me.

"A nurse's aid just gave Fremont a cold shower. Come on, let's get out of here." And while Harvey cracked up, we both dashed for the elevator.

On the way home Harvey laughed so hard after I explained all the details that he nearly drove off the road. "I knew this would be great!" Harv roared. "Wait till I tell Beaver!"

Wait till I call Janice, I thought. I hoped I hadn't gotten her into trouble. But in fact, Janice started laughing again when I called her later that night.

"It was a scream," she said. "I never laughed so hard at anything. You should hear the nurses, they're all laughing about it, too—*now*. Really, Jamie, it was better than a Three Stooges comedy. Honest."

Well, I don't know about that. But it sure was a rush. Poor Fremont crawled around in a frenzy in his container for over an hour, and he wouldn't even touch a cricket for dinner. I guess it really shook the poor guy up.

CHAPTER 11

Within the next couple of days Fremont sort of became a legend around old Glenwood High. Harv, then Beaver, then others began describing the "tarantula incident," as it came to be called, at St. Joseph's Hospital. No one mentioned the fact that we went there to cheer up Janice. Somehow in the course of describing the story, all Harvey mentioned was the gorgeous nurse he was "dealing" while I set Fremont loose in the hallway. Anyway, I started getting all kinds of kids coming up to me and asking about my spider and when was I going to bring him to school for a visit.

One really good thing came out of Fremont's visit to the hospital. I guess Janice got such a surge of adrenaline—that's a chemical in your body that keeps you going—that the doctors said it "facilitated a loosening of the mucus clogging her respiratory system." Janice said that meant she got a lot of the gunk out faster and could go home sooner.

While those things were happening, Ginger and I began our dance lessons. Now, I couldn't dance worth anything! I mean "two left feet" and all those other sayings applied to me because I'm just basically uncoordinated. But taking dancing lessons with Ginger was definitely enjoyable—and she really did teach me how to dance, too.

Our first night of lessons, she said, "OK, Jamie, let's just see how you get down and boogie," and she put on something fast. Watching Ginger was great, but she was watching me, too, and pretty soon she was hysterical.

"Jamie, you look like a giraffe with a bad case of lumbago! This'll never do. Hey, let's try some slow ones."

That's when I really started enjoying myself.

"One, two, three, four; come on—just like you're dancing in a box," she instructed. And pretty soon I was getting the hang of it. Holding on tight to Ginger made it difficult to concentrate on my dance steps, though.

I kept cracking Ginger up by repeating the numbers out loud to keep time. Ginger instructed, "Don't count out loud. Listen, just look into my eyes while we dance, OK? That's it. Good."

And it worked! I just kept looking into her eyes, and pretty soon I was in perfect step.

But while we were dancing to another slow one and I was looking into her eyes, something came over me. I gently stopped her, still holding her in my arms, and kissed her. I didn't maul her or slobber all over her like washing a car. I just kissed her softly on the lips.

She looked at me for a moment or two, and I thought, well, the party's over. "Sorry," I whispered, and sort of hung my head down.

But she lifted up my chin. "Don't be." She smiled. And we continued dancing.

While I was drifting off into ecstasy, Ginger asked, "Jamie, who is she?"

Then *I* stopped dancing. "Who's who?"

Ginger went on, "You know, your sick friend. You told me you called her at school a few days ago. You did say 'her,' remember?"

"Yeah," I mumbled.

"Well, who is she?" Ginger asked. She didn't seem angry. In fact, it seemed like curiosity more than anything else.

"Janice Brooks," I said.

"Janice. The skinny little girl in my chemistry class?"

"Yeah."

"So that's why she's been absent so much," she said, almost to herself. "Cystic fibrosis." She looked at me. "That's why you and Harvey went to that hospital the other night?"

I nodded my head.

"That's really . . . I don't know, that's really kind."

"She's a good friend," I said.

We danced a few slow ones before I went home.

"Think I'll be ready to try some faster ones the next time?" I asked as I got ready to leave.

"For sure," she replied. "But I think we can work on some slow ones, too," she added with a wink.

"I can't wait," I said.

* * *

"What do you mean you can't make it tonight? Whatsa matter, ain't we good enough to hang around with anymore?" On our way to school, Harvey was chewing me out for not having been over during the last three days.

"Harv, I got a previous engagement," I said.

"Who with, Toothpick?" the Beaver chimed in.

"Her name is Janice, Bucky Beaver!" I snapped.

"OK, OK. Janice. Who cares?"

"I can't make it because Ginger and I are getting together," I explained.

"Again?" Harv asked, knowing about my previous lessons.

But I didn't get over to Ginger's right away. After I got home, my mother was sitting at the kitchen table, peeling potatoes and giving me a funny look while I grabbed an apple from the refrigerator.

I gave her a quizzical look in return and said, "What's the matter? I washed my hands before I opened the fridge."

She shook her head. "You got another phone call from a girl," she announced, saying it with all the joy she'd use for "You got another D in English."

"Is that OK?" I asked.

"Well, what happened to you, Harvey, and Rick? You used to get together every afternoon."

"Things have sort of changed, Mom," I replied. She still had a troubled look on her face, but there didn't seem to be anything else to say. I didn't really understand what was happening, and I knew I couldn't begin to explain to my parents, either.

"Who called?" I suddenly remembered.

"Janice. She asked you to call her at home."

After I grabbed the cordless phone and rushed to my room, I called. "Janice? You're home!"

"Yeah," came a dismal reply.

"Can you have visitors?" I asked.

"Sure. But you can't stay for long."

"That's all right. I just wanna see you, that's all." Even though I'd called her a couple of times in the last few days, I hadn't gone to see her. After Fremont and I came calling, we decided that would be best. The hospital was cool about the incident; maybe they just didn't want to get sued because they'd let me and a tarantula into Janice's room. Anyway, they never mentioned a thing to Janice's parents, and, of course, I never told mine.

When Mrs. Brooks took me to Janice's room, Janice gave me a big smile from her bed, where she was propped up on a bunch of pillows. But the smile soon faded, and I knew something was wrong.

We talked a little about school and what she had to make up for classes, but it wasn't the same. I mean, she just wasn't the cheerful person she always had been.

"What's wrong?" I asked.

Janice only looked at me with a sad expression. "I guess this is one of the bad days. Something you haven't seen me have," she explained.

I wrinkled my eyebrows, not sure what she meant.

"Oh, Jamie. Sometimes it's easy to pretend—or put so

many things in motion you don't have time to think about it." She grabbed the covers tightly in her frail hands, and slowly a tear rolled down one cheek. "You see ... I'm dying," she whispered. "And it's just not acceptable to me. I don't think—" And then she rolled over in her bed, away from me, and began to cry.

I sat there a few moments. At first I felt like I couldn't move or speak, but then I began slowly, "I don't think it's fair, either.

"Janice? Can I tell you a story?" When she sat up again I told her about Arnold "Cheeseburger" and all his misfortunes, and the day Norris Pendowski decided that was enough, that it wasn't fair. I ended by saying, "I guess life isn't very fair, is it?" She barely shook her head.

A few moments later Janice looked up and asked, "Would you do me a favor?"

"Of course."

"Every day I'm not at school, write down what you see happening during classes, at lunch, on the bus—whatever. Then you can read me your notes, or stuff them in my mailbox if I'm too ill, just so I know what's happening.

"I get so tired of staring at four walls. Jamie, you're sensitive to people and things. You could be my roving reporter at school when I'm not there."

"OK." It was the first time I'd seen Janice cry. It shook me, I guess; she had always been so positive about everything. So, if writing a crazy daily report for her would help, I was going to do it.

Wednesday, March 24

Dear Janice,

My mother just ran off with a lion tamer, my father's in love with a gypsy, and my cousin flushed my pet tarantula down the toilet. Can you help me? OOPS! Sorry, Janice. I guess I got carried away there—although my letter is probably far more entertaining than a review of *The Rhyme of the Ancient Mariner*, which we're *still* reading in Balkler's class. ZZZZZZZZZZZ ... Uh, sorry. Did I doze off again? You know, I never realized how many people snored until I took this class....

And on it went. Any day Janice was absent, I kept her posted on current events at Glenwood. Like Harvey missing breakfast and then wolfing down two platefuls of the cafeteria's notorious "barfaroni"—which completely grossed out everybody at the table where we were sitting. Or during gym class when two guys poured lighter fluid on Rick's jockstrap, set it on fire, and threw it at him while we were taking our showers. You know—just the little things that sort of break up the routine at school.

I saved my note-taking for appropriate times—like during Balkler's class, where almost everybody was asleep anyway, or in Art and Music Appreciation, so that Harv and Beaver never saw what I was working on.

Janice really enjoyed "The Glenwood Report," as she soon called it. She put all my notes in a white folder after I dropped them off at her house, and wrote in her own comments in green ink in the margins.

When Janice made it to school—which was less and less often—we'd share the writing duties. Some classes we didn't have together, so she'd write her observations for me to read, like:

> Chemistry I, 3rd hour: Jamie, did you know we can use Avogadro's Principle to show elemental gases are diatomic? Awesome, huh?
>
> Who cares? Hi, Jamie!
>
> The above contribution is from Ginger. Anyway, if we assume hydrogen and chlorine are monatomic, their reaction would be $H + Cl = HCl$! Thrilling, isn't it? Blah!

That was the kind of stuff Janice would write. What a brain—she could talk about elemental diatomic whatcha-macallits and still try to crack a joke.

We really had some fun with our journal. And when she was home, Janice had something she could read and reread. She told me that meant a lot.

CHAPTER 12

The Sadie Hawkins Dance was on a Friday night. I persuaded my dad to let me borrow our "new" car for the occasion. It's not really new. In fact, it's a two-year-old Cutlass, but he hardly ever drives it. Instead, we mainly use our '77 VW; it's a two-tone—yellow and rust. My dad proudly says, "It's got ninety-seven thousand miles on it and still going strong!" Anyway, I convinced him that Ginger would be far more impressed with the "new" car, with its all-white interior still looking and smelling like new.

"Are you serious about this girl, son?" he asked.

"Naw," I muttered.

"Well, just don't take her too seriously."

I almost said, "What?" But thought better of it. Why risk a long discussion on females with Dad when he was already going to lend me the car? Right?

During the day on Friday, Harv and Rick would hardly speak to me; I guess they were jealous. Even a few guys I hardly knew said, "Ginger's takin' *you* to the dance?" You know, like I was the Elephant Man or something.

My mom dug a pair of old bibbed overalls out of a trunk in the attic; she said my grandfather wore them when he worked on the railroads in Ohio. I put them on along with an old flannel shirt and a yellow cap that read *Farm-All Tractors*. I figured that was hokey enough, but my dad persuaded me to wear the old work boots I use when I walk Benny in the winter. I think I looked more like a reject from the local truck drivers' school than a farmer!

I had the car keys in my hand and was heading for the door when the phone rang. Thinking it might be Ginger with some last-minute instructions, I picked up the phone.

"Hello? Oh, hello, Mrs. Brooks." I almost knew what to expect. She quickly explained that they had just driven Janice to the hospital, and she knew I would want to know.

"Does Janice want me to call her?" I asked.

"Oh, she doesn't even know I'm calling, Jamie," she replied.

"Thanks, Mrs. Brooks. I'm glad you called."

"Anything wrong?" my dad asked.

"No . . . I mean, yeah. Janice Brooks is back in the hospital." I had explained to my parents a couple of nights before about Janice and cystic fibrosis. They were really sympathetic. My dad told me I had real character to be helpful like that to someone so ill. I almost tried to explain it had been the other way around—Janice helping me— but it was too complicated.

"Try to have a good time anyway, son," he said. "I'm sure you'll be able to call her over the weekend."

"Thanks, Dad. I'll see ya later."

What perfect timing! I'm sure Janice's mom knew nothing about tonight's dance and Janice hadn't asked her to call. It just worked out that way.

There I was. Driving over to Ginger's—our first real date—but I was already bummed out because Janice was sick again.

Ginger looked scrumptious! She had on an old-timey dress with an apron, but it was kind of cut low in front. I mean it was definitely an eye-grabber.

"How do I look?" she asked.

"Gorgeous!"

After she looked me over, she started laughing. "You really got dressed for the part!"

"That bad?" I said grimly.

"No, I like it," she said, putting her arm through mine. "You look cute. Shall we go?"

"Cute, huh?" I said, backing out of her driveway and trying to catch a glimpse of myself in the rear-view mirror.

I think I had more fun driving Ginger to the school and during our ride home than at the dance. By ourselves we laughed and joked together, but at the dance . . . well, I just didn't feel at ease.

They had bales of hay stacked here and there in the gym and something called a "bluegrass" band doing the music. Mr. Kellog was there in blue jeans and a straw hat, "marrying" couples for two dollars. Ginger and I got married, had our picture taken, got some Cokes, and sat on a bale of hay, waiting for the band to play a slow one.

Let me tell you, I'm glad we don't have to sit on straw

all the time. After a while I started itching in places you don't normally scratch in public.

"Jamie," Ginger whispered, "I can't stand sitting on this stuff."

"Me, either."

"Let's walk around," she said, taking my hand.

As luck would have it, the first couples we ran into were Jerome and his date, Lois Fielder. Lois is pretty, but she's always covering her mouth when she smiles because of her braces. Skeeter Thomas and his girl had double-dated with the Hump. "You look really sharp, Ginger," the Hump declared. Then he turned his attention to me. "You were supposed to dress like a farmer, James—not wear your school clothes," he said with a deadly smile while Skeeter smirked.

"Hey, man! I thought it was a formal," I replied. Everybody laughed except Jerome.

Then a slow one began, so Ginger and I decided to test out my dancing ability.

I did pretty well, too. I didn't even have to count "one, two, three, four" out loud. I just said it to myself.

At one point during the dance, when Ginger excused herself to go to the powder room, I decided to go down to the office and see if the phone booths were open. The halls were dark, so I could make my call in private. I had to know how Janice was—just let her know I was thinking of her.

The booths were empty, so I parked myself in one, closed the folding door, and took a deep breath of good old stale phone booth air.

I could make out St. Joe's number where I had scratched it on the wall. I had picked the right booth. I wondered if Janice could possibly be in the same room.

After I dialed, her unmistakable voice rasped, "Hello?"

"Janice?" I said.

"Jamie? Is that you?" she quickly responded. "How did you know?"

"Never mind. How are you?"

"Well . . ." She hesitated. "Things aren't real good right now."

There was a painful silence. I didn't know what to say. After a few moments she asked, "Jamie, what about the dance?"

"It's been OK so far."

"You mean you're there?" She laughed.

"Yeah. I guess I pick weird times to call you, huh?"

"I don't care. I'm glad you did." Then suddenly, "Uh-oh, gotta go, I'm not supposed to be talking now."

"I'll call you later," I said.

"OK."

Ginger was standing at the gym entrance, obviously looking for me.

"Where were you?" she asked.

"Nature called," I explained.

"Have trouble finding the little boys' room?" She giggled.

"Yeah! I mean those halls are dark and scary," I joked.

Ginger laughed. I liked the way she laughed and smiled and put her arm through mine.

"Shall we return to the party?" I sighed.

"Why not?" she replied.

As we walked together into the gym, I got a dirty look from some dude who obviously didn't think I was worthy of beautiful Ginger Gregson, but I didn't let it bother me.

CHAPTER 13

Janice came home a lot sooner than I thought she would, and I guess a lot sooner than her parents wanted her to. But she was serious about not going back to the hospital, not unless she was dying or something.

Pretty soon her dad was driving her to school and picking her up after her last class. I guess he left work early to drive her home. That's how concerned he was. That way she didn't have to walk those blocks to the bus stop or home. It might not sound like much, but Janice was really frail. She even used a little backpack to carry her books in because her arms had become too weak to hold them. Whenever I could, I carried her books for her. It wasn't much, but I wanted to do what I could.

Janice always kept smiling, and her positive attitude didn't change. "Gee, I'm glad to be at school," she admitted one day after I complained about an upcoming geometry test.

And you know, I understood what she meant, too. After seeing her so down that one night, and hearing about how much she hated staring at four walls all the time, I knew she was glad to be with people, even if it meant going to school. I guess unless you've been sick like that you really don't understand.

Those days she was at school, we still kept writing in "The Glenwood Report." In fact, Janice and I were happily discussing it as we walked to her next class when the big blowout occurred. I guess trouble had been brewing for a while. Like Hump, Harv, and Rick, a few other guys were ticked off because Ginger and I had become friends. So one of them, a Glenwood tough guy named Rory Soper, decided to give me a hassle.

Janice was telling me how we should collect all our stories together and make it into a book.

"Into a book? Are you kiddin', Janice?"

"No," she said seriously, but Janice never got to finish.

We were just about to start up the stairs to the second floor when Soper called out, "Hey, Needle, whatcha walkin' around with Toothpick for? I thought Ginger was your chicky-poo?"

Right away I felt my guts tightening. The way he said it, and the way I felt, I knew there would be trouble.

"Her name's Janice," I replied, feeling my mouth go dry. I stared at Rory, who was leaning against the lockers with some other clowns. He had a wicked smile on his face. Because Janice and I had stopped at the bottom of the stairs, the flow of students going either way got jammed up. But everybody got real quiet when Rory stepped closer to me and said, "I say her name is Toothpick, faggot!"

Although Janice grabbed my arm and said, "Jamie, please, let's go," everything sort of went crazy. I let our books slip out of my arms, my head buzzing, and slammed my right fist into Soper's face with all my might.

Right away there were shouts and yells from everyone around us. I'm no fighter, and I'm sure everybody—including me—thought I was going to get murdered, but I couldn't stand there letting him say those things.

My punch was lucky. I caught him on the nose, and he banged his head against a locker. With blood pouring from one nostril, he came at me like a madman. I only got in one more good hit before it was all his fight.

After getting pounded in the face a couple of times, I ducked into a boxer's crouch with my arms up, trying not to get hurt too bad. Kids were packed in so close around us that when somebody grabbed my neck like in a vise, I thought it might be a student. But the punching stopped at the same time, and I heard a voice boom:

"It's all over, guys! Come on with me. I'm sure Purdick will be glad to see your face again, Soper!"

Good old Mr. Stout, our football coach, had a powerful hand around each of our necks and was literally dragging us to the office. Stout's arms are bigger than my thighs, so it was an easy exercise for him.

When he delivered us to the office, he looked at Soper's bloody nose, smiled, and then turned to me.

"Almont?" he uttered in amazement, and then shook his head.

One of my eyes was swelling, and I could feel my upper lip puffing out, so I offered no reply.

Stout gave our principal, Mr. Purdick, the story. After that, Soper was called into the principal's office, and Purdick proceeded to read him the riot act.

A lot of kids were still outside the office, pressing their hands and noses against the glass. I avoided looking at them until I heard Harvey's unmistakable voice.

When I turned, Harv sort of gaped in astonishment. "You?" He mouthed the word while pointing a finger at me.

That's what Purdick said when it was my turn to enter his office. "You, Almont?" he asked in surprise.

"Sit down," he instructed. Twirling a pencil between his fingers, he gazed at me as if he had just been informed I'd assassinated Ayatollah Khomeini.

"Jamie, you have epitomized the quiet kind of student who never gives anyone any hassle, so consequently I rarely see you. And now this! What possessed you to pick a fight with Rory Soper and give him a bloody nose?"

I explained as best as I could about my feelings about Janice and cystic fibrosis, that she was thin because of it, that I'd had it with people being called names like Toothpick, Cheeseburger, and all the rest, and today Soper had passed the breaking point. "I just saw red and started swinging, I guess," I ended.

Mr. Purdick sat way back in his chair. He listened to everything I said, never interrupting.

"That's all very admirable, Jamie. I truly mean it. Unfortunately, we do not allow fighting in school, so I'm suspending you for the next three days."

I knew that was coming. Unavoidable, I guess. Still, when he called my mom and she had to drive to school and pick me up, I felt like I was being shipped off to a leper colony or something. My only consolation was Soper's getting a five-day suspension because he'd been in so many fights before.

The ride home was painfully quiet. I guess my mom was in shock after the principal called to give her the glad tidings. Before we got in the car, she said she didn't want to discuss matters until my dad got home.

I headed for my bedroom with an ice pack Mom had gotten me. It was really gloomy outside; another spring storm was brewing, but that pretty much fit my mood. After I greeted Fremont with a friendly tap against his glass container, I got the fish food out to feed my tropicals. But before I dropped the flakes in the water, I noticed one of my black-laced angelfish floating lifelessly near the bottom. One of my algae eaters took a nip at his fins. He was very dead.

After I fished his body out of the tank with my net, I took his remains to the backyard and flung them on the spot where my dad plants a garden each summer. No, I wasn't thinking he'd be great fertilizer: I just can't stand flushing fish down the toilet. It grosses me out. I got in the house just before a downpour began.

When Dad got home I could hear him and my mom discussing the news in hushed voices. It was still raining, and I was lying on my side on the bed reading the latest copy of *Creepy Creatures* magazine, when my dad opened the door.

"Hi, Dad," I said soberly, closing the magazine.

He leaned in the doorway and sighed. "Had some trouble at school today, huh?" he began.

"Yeah, I guess so."

"Wanna tell me about it?"

"Gee, Dad, didn't Mom tell ya what happened?"

"She told me what the principal said, but I wanted to hear it from you," he said gently.

I stared at the high-gloss shine on my bedroom floor. "This guy called Janice and me some names," I began. "I mean, he was really nasty. I guess I just lost my cool and let him have it."

"Looks like he let you have it, too," my father smiled, eyeing my battle scars.

"Yeah. A fighter I'm not."

We were quiet a few moments, listening to the aquarium gurgling, when he said, "Well, fighting rarely resolves a situation. But sometimes a punk like that can push you too far. I want you to realize that if you start a fight, you better be ready to finish it." He paused a moment, "Well, that's what my father told me once after I got worked over."

We both started to laugh in spite of my swollen lip. I hadn't laughed at anything all afternoon.

"Maybe you should check with us before you go anywhere, until you get back to school."

"OK, Dad." He closed the door.

When the phone rang I knew who it would be. After I

took the phone in my room, I said, "Hello?"

"Hey, is this the home of Muhammad Ali?" Harvey laughed.

"Thanks, Harv. Whatcha call for, to give me some tips on boxing?" I asked sarcastically.

"No, man! I told you, I'm your friend. Hey, I took care of your girlfriends for you today."

"What?" Instantly I thought of Janice. What had she done after the fight?

"Yeah. I picked up your books and Janice's and walked her to her class. I even asked her if she wanted me to come back and walk her to her next class." Since Harvey never carries books of his own, it wasn't a major feat of strength or inconvenience.

"Was she OK?" I asked.

"Oh no, she was cryin', man. But I told her not to worry— if he only hit you in the face, then there couldn't be too much damage." Good old Harv. His sense of humor is so bad that if somebody set you on fire, Harv would laugh and say, "Hey, got a light?"

"Thanks for carrying her books, Harv."

"That's all right. I'll just put it on your bill. Hey, I also sat next to Ginger on the bus and let her cry on my shoulder on the way home. She was real worried about ya."

"Gee, Harv, you're a pal." I groaned.

"Hey, not that I want you to worry or nothin', but guys that punch out Rory Soper don't usually live too long. You plannin' on leavin' town?"

"Yeah. I'm leaving on a banana boat for Brazil in the

morning. Listen, I'll talk to you later."

"OK, hit man!" He laughed again.

I took Benny for a long walk after supper. When I got back, we were both pretty muddy from the rain, but my mom didn't make the usual fuss about tracking dirt through the house. I guess she realized there were other things to worry about.

I had to call Janice. I'd been thinking of what to say to her while walking the dog.

Mrs. Brooks answered the phone. She told me Janice was coughing a lot and mentioned something about the horrid weather. Janice could only speak to me for a minute.

She sounded really bad. "Janice, are you all right?" I asked.

"What about you?" she answered in a scratchy voice and then began coughing.

"I'm OK. Really. My parents aren't ticked off or anything, but I got suspended."

She was still coughing but managed to say, "I'm sorry."

"Janice, I'm sorry, too. And I wish . . . I just wish you felt better."

"Thanks," she rasped. Then her mom came on the line and said I'd better try calling later.

I sat in the room brooding. Looking at my tropical fish swimming gracefully in their tank, I suddenly wished I were one of them. No feelings, no worries. Just wait for the food flakes to come floating down; and when you croak, no fuss, no muss—just a scoop of the net and out you go.

"Jamie," I heard my mother call. "There's someone in the driveway."

"What now?" I said to myself as I walked into the living room. My parents were both standing at the window, looking at an old beat-up car with a couple of guys sitting in front. Because of the rain and their headlights, we couldn't make out who was inside.

"If this is any kind of trouble, Jamie, I'll handle it," my father said.

But when one of the guys got out of the car and came walking toward the porch, I said, "Don't worry. Gee, I can't believe it. It's Norris Pendowski!"

Before my parents could say, *"Who?,"* Norris was at the door. After I let him in, he just stood there dripping on my mom's carpet and nodded curtly to my parents. Then he said to me, "I just wanted you to know I had a little talk with that guy Rory Soper. And I says to him, next time I might hafta even things up. You know what I mean?"

I nodded my head, "Yeah. I gotcha."

"So . . . I'll see ya later." Then he walked back to the car and drove away, never once speaking to my parents.

My mom had a horrified look on her face, and Dad said, "What was that all about?"

"It's a long story, Dad." I smiled. "But it's OK."

I couldn't talk to Janice for the next three days. Her mom said she was in something called an ICU. So I wrote a lot of stuff in our journal to take to her when I could.

I tried to make it funny. When I described Norris's visit

to our house, I wrote that my dad asked, "Who *was* that masked man?" I even tried drawing a picture of Fremont, but he ended up looking like an octopus wearing a red and brown fur coat. Oh well, so much for art! Ginger called me twice after school. That was the highlight of my suspension. And Harv came over to watch the Stooges with me to help pass the time.

By Monday I was back in school. Somehow things felt different. Like Beaver was trying his hardest to be friendly, and in the lunch line when I bumped into the Hump, he turned and said, "Hey, Jamie, how ya doin'?"

The best part, though, was seeing Ginger at school again and walking with her to Kellog's class. I was actually glad to be back!

When I got home that afternoon, my mom told me that Mrs. Brooks had called her and wanted me to come and see Janice as soon as I could. Mom had a real somber look when she said it, so I grabbed our journal. My mom handed me the car keys, and I was off to St. Joseph's.

I found out what the ICU is. Janice was in the Intensive Care Unit, with all kinds of machines and nurses floating around. They said I could only see her for fifteen minutes.

"Hi, Jamie," she rasped with a smile, while this plastic thing over her mouth fed her oxygen. She looked bad. Her eyes seemed to have shrunk into her head, and her skin looked like wax. When I took hold of her hand, it felt cool.

I passed her our journal, and she thanked me. Then we just sat there looking at each other, listening to her struggle for breath through the machine.

"This summer we're gonna start on that book," I finally said, trying desperately to cheer her—and myself—up. She smiled and gently nodded her head.

"You'll have to go now," a nurse whispered a little later.

"I'll come again, as soon as they'll let me. I'll see ya," I said as positively as I could.

In the lobby her mother said, "Thank you so much for coming, Jamie." I felt kind of awkward because Mrs. Brooks looked like she'd been crying, and Janice's father seemed pretty upset, too.

After I left, I just drove out into the country for a long, long time. My parents didn't say anything when I got back. Mom had kept my supper warm, but I told her I wasn't hungry, and went to my room.

Have you ever felt so empty you can't speak or think at all? That's how I felt as I lay on my bed gazing at the ceiling. I don't even remember falling asleep.

When the phone rang the next morning, I thought it might be my father's alarm, but when I looked at my clock, I knew it was too early to be that.

I listened to him get out of bed and answer the phone. He didn't say much, but I could make out, "I'm terribly sorry, Mrs. Brooks," before he hung up.

A few moments later he tapped at my door. "I know, Dad," I barely managed to say.

I'm glad I didn't go to school that day. Mr. Purdick announced Janice's death over the P.A. in the morning and asked for a moment of silence. Anyway, that's what Harvey told me when he called that afternoon. "I guess I'll see ya at the funeral home this evening, then," he said somberly. "I'm gonna wear my blue suit."

Ginger called, too. "Oh, Jamie, I'm so sorry," she said. Ginger told me that the student council was going to send flowers.

A bit later on, Mrs. Brooks came to our front door. My mom and I were sort of lost for words. She was very pleasant, despite the hurt look in her eyes.

"I can only stay a moment," she said, "we still have so much to do.

"Jamie, I know Janice wanted you to have this," and she handed me our journal, "The Glenwood Report," and said slowly, "That meant so much to her. And you meant so much to her."

We stood there a few moments in awkward silence before Mrs. Brooks said, "I really must go now. Good-bye."

After Mom closed the door, I slowly walked to my room, carrying the journal Mrs. Brooks had given me. I sat on the bed thumbing through the pages, thinking about the times we had laughed at some of our entries.

Janice had written a few lines on the last page along with some doodling kind of pictures. Near the bottom of the page were the day, the month, and year—yesterday, the day she died.

Under the date she had written: "*All* that I ever want you to know, Jamie, is be *good* to yourself. Love, Toothpick." Then she'd drawn a little happy face under it.

I looked at that for a while. Then I got a pen from my desk and finished our journal. Under Janice's happy face I wrote: "Jamie loves Toothpick."

I closed the folder and put it on the shelf between last year's yearbook and my favorite albums.

"Mom, I'm taking Benny for a walk," I said as I headed out the door.

We ran all the way to the fields at the back of our subdivision. We'd gone about a half-mile, into the tall grass toward the woods, before I started to cry.